HODGE

NORMAN ABRAHAMSON

This book is dedicated to my parents,
Paul and Elaine, who made me a reader,
and Leslie, Matt and David, who put up with a writer.

1. Road Trip

The slam of the auctioneer's gavel sliced through me like a knife. My knees shook and then buckled. It was all gone: my job, my children, my wife, and now my house and possessions. All I had were my memories, and I was not so sure I could trust them. At seventy-four years of age, I, George Wellington Hodge, PhD. English Literature, Professor Emeritus, of The College of the Holy Cross of Worcester Massachusetts, was homeless.

I retired from teaching on May 27, 1996 after grading more than seven thousand final exams for Introduction to Shakespeare. I never thought it proper to allow teaching assistants to grade essay exams. The rank and file of teaching assistants assigned to me principally consisted of graduate students who would ultimately fail to complete their doctoral requirements. That's quite all right if they are checking over calculus examinations which leave no room for personal interpretation as to the correct answer, but it is quite another thing to allow a teaching assistant, whose greatest scholarly accomplishment is the ability to scrape together tuition year after year, to determine how well another student understands and writes about Shakespeare, or anything else for that matter.

Immediately after retirement, I began my new full time job, caring for my wife, Katherine. Katherine and I were married in 1946, less than one year after my discharge from the army and only five months after we first met. Kat's formal education ended with high school, but she shared my passion for reading, especially the classics. Shakespeare was her favorite. She enjoyed the plays, but it was his poetry and sonnets that truly captured her soul. Shortly before my retirement, Katherine began getting absent minded. When I retired Kat could recite with absolute accuracy Portia's plea to Shylock for mercy on behalf of the indebted Antonio. She could not, however, remember where she had put her shoes, or the best route to take from our bedroom to the bathroom.

Alzheimer's relentlessly robbed Kat of her identity one memory at a time. Her doctor suggested that I put her in a nursing home, where she would be attended by strangers. I was quite appalled at the suggestion. My wedding vows specifically mentioned "for better and for worse, in sickness and in health." Do the betrothed even listen to their vows anymore? Why do so many people ignore the meaning of the words they use? Perhaps folks today don't pay attention even to themselves. The attention span of my final class of students was slightly shorter than the length of the average television commercial. These days nobody even expects a person to mean what they say unless a lawyer is present.

Excuse the digression. I was telling you about Kat. As I said, we swore to love and support each other even in sickness, and for worse as well as better. Most of our fifty-two years and ten months together were damn good. We had our tragedies, as most people do, and we struggled through them together. How could I desert her when she needed me most? Even if she could not remember our life together, I could.

I remember when I broke my back in 1962. I was up on a ladder painting our house on Meadow View Road. That's the same house Kat died in. My son rode his bicycle into the ladder which knocked the paint can, paint brush and me, into space. As I fell toward the ground I saw the horrified look on my boy's face. At that moment, we both thought that he had killed me. I put my hands out in an attempt to break my fall. I broke my arms instead. And my back. I was in bed for six months. During that time Kat nursed me to health while she contended with two quarrelsome children. She never complained, at least not to me.

So I did not complain about caring for Kat. Why should I? What good would it do? When you love a woman, as I loved Kat, it is your privilege to do for her what you are able to do. Alzheimer's disease does not get better, and it takes a long time to do its job. I hired nurses to be in the home around the clock. I hired contractors to build a bathroom right off of our bedroom. Handles were installed in the tub and by the toilet so Kat could use them without difficulty. I had doors installed to block off the stairway the morning after Kat fell down the stairs in a state of confusion.

Kat got worse. She began to suffer from a variety of ailments, one after another. Pneumonia, phlebitis, shingles, a collapsed lung, kidney stones: the list went on and on and with it, associated expenses. I took out a mortgage on our home to pay all the nurses, doctors, contractors, hospitals, and finally, the funeral home. I had long since spent everything saved in our IRA accounts. The social security benefits of $1,255.00 per month I received did not cover the mortgage. My car fell into disrepair and I could not afford to get it fixed. I sold it to my mechanic for two hundred and fifty dollars.

I suppose I should have tried to sell the house, but I

had planned to die in my home. Unfortunately, I miscalculated my life expectancy. I fell behind on the mortgage, and the bank did what banks do; it foreclosed the mortgage.

As stubborn as I am, even I knew my house would be taken from me. I applied for admission to an elderly housing complex in Worcester. I found myself on the wrong end of a three year waiting list. Not only had I foolishly outlived my wife, I had tragically outlived my children. I had no place to move my possessions, nor the money to put them in storage. I would not sell them. I left everything at home except the valise with two suits and some changes of underwear that I brought out with me. I still imagine that my house is exactly as I left it, furnished with the chairs, beds, desks, sofas, bookcases and bureaus collected by Kat and me over our lifetimes. I know, of course, that it is not so, but it comforts me to imagine it.

When my house was sold at foreclosure auction on February 17, 1998, the buyer paid exactly what I owed the bank on the mortgage note, interest, as well as the costs and attorney's fees that were tacked on. As a result, there would be no surplus funds to be turned over to me. The foreclosure system is nothing if not efficient.

Worcester, Massachusetts in February is damn cold. Worcester is also perhaps the windiest city in the contiguous forty-eight states. The wind whips up and down the roller coaster hills of the city turning trash and ice chips into projectiles. I picked up my valise and walked downtown to the Aurora Hotel, where generations of Holy Cross boys had brought their less reputable dates. After most of seventy-four years, I spent my last night in the City of Worcester, Massachusetts, on a lumpy mattress in the Aurora Hotel. Kat would have laughed.

The next morning I checked out and began my trek to Florida. Why Florida? Isn't that where old people go to die? I have seen scores of friends and family members move to Florida over the years. That is where men who have spent their lives wearing a suit and tie every day suddenly wear loose, pastel, button-down shirts; long Bermuda shorts; black socks and sandals. Their wives take to wearing stretch slacks with a pull over cotton shirt or sweatshirt covered with rhinestones. I believe that Florida is America's answer to the mythical elephant graveyard. It is as good a place as any to go...to die. I've heard it called, God's waiting room. Why not check in?

I no longer had a mailing address or a forwarding address. As a result, the Social Security Administration would not send my social security checks until I could prove to them that I am me, and that I am here, and that here has a mailing address. I decided to get to Florida the only way I could afford, by thumb. I had not hitchhiked since I was in the army but was certain I remembered how. I assumed that a well-dressed, elderly man would be unthreatening enough to garner a ride in fairly short order. I was wrong. Sometimes I forget how much America has changed in the past fifty years. The time went by so fast.

I struck out from the Aurora at 6:15 A.M. I was wearing a brown wool suit over a white button down long sleeve shirt and a brown paisley tie. I wore a heavy black wool overcoat and scarf topped off with a fur hat and was held fast to the ground by green rubber boots into which I tucked my pant legs. My shoes were in my valise. There was no point in ruining my black leather Florsheims in the salty gray slush that collects on the sides of roads in winter. The icy gutter soup freezes feet and leaves permanent white stains on shoe leather. I had fifty dollars in my billfold, and seven hundred and fifty-six dollars hidden in the lining of my overcoat. I was, of course, clean shaven.

I have always been a terrific walker. I suppose that I am built for it. Even at seventy-four years old I was still six feet, two inches tall. I had never weighed more than one hundred and eighty pounds, but my weight had dropped to one hundred and fifty- five. Nevertheless, my long legs still had their full stride and worked as tirelessly as they ever had. Kat and I had gone on a walking tour of rural Great Britain twenty years before. We walked for miles each day carrying our canvas rucksacks. Walking along Main Street in downtown Worcester, and then east on Route 9, reminded me of a time when I was young, vibrant and healthy, and I felt a sense of adventure and excitement for the first time in a decade.

Each day of the previous four years had been all too predictable. Wake up at five- thirty and prepare a bath for Kat. Remove Kat's soiled underclothing and bed sheets for washing while I bathed Kat. Feed Kat breakfast. Take her to the bathroom every hour so she would not soil herself. Prepare lunch while a nurse took Kat's blood pressure and temperature and administered the prescriptions of the day. And talk. I talked to Kat all day. I would tell her about our children, our trips, our life together. Usually, she responded with a quizzical look, but every so often she would smile and remember an incident or even add something to a story. Then, as quickly as she remembered, she forgot.

Now I was beginning a new day with no idea of what might occur! A healthy sense of adventure can compensate for a host of physical discomforts. I walked up and down the hills of Route 9, leaning into the wind until I crossed the Worcester City Limits at the bridge over Lake Quinsigamond. Then I turned around, put my valise in my left hand, and stuck out my thumb. As rush hour was getting underway, cars and trucks sped past me. Although many drivers turned in their seat to stare at me and shake a disapproving head, none were inclined to stop during my first half hour of hitchhiking. The wind from the east blew against my back, and the passing traffic blew an exhaust laden current into my face. I was not, however, discouraged. There were times, when I was in the service, that I'd had to stand in one place for hours while waiting for a ride.

My eyes watered copiously from the wind and fumes,

turning the traffic into a multi-colored blur. Finally, a car pulled over and I opened the door to get inside. My first ride! I was now *officially* on my way to Florida. I wiped my eyes and thanked the driver, who was not nearly as friendly as I would have hoped.

"What do you think you're doing getting into a police car, pal? Have you been drinking?" asked the driver. That was the first time I ever spoke to a policeman from Shrewsbury.

"Excuse me, officer. My eyes are watering and I didn't notice that this is a police car. Does this mean that you aren't going to give me a ride?" I asked.

"Listen, pal, it's against the law to hitchhike. It's also dangerous. You're lucky you didn't get run over, standing in the right lane like you were. Did your car break down somewhere?"

"No, officer. I don't own a car anymore."

"Well, where do you live? Maybe I can give you a lift home."

"I don't have a home, officer. I'm moving."

"To where?"

"Florida."

"You plan on hitchhiking to Florida?"

"Yes."

"Forget it. I'm going to have to arrest you. Get in the back seat."

"Really? This is turning into quite an interesting day."

The officer grunted in response and shook his head. He got out of the car and walked around to my side. He opened the door and pulled me out. Then he quickly frisked me right there on the street and put me in the back seat. My valise was left on the front seat. When he got back into the car and put it into drive he spoke to me again.

"What is your name, sir?"

"George Wellington Hodge. What is your name, officer?"

"Rogers."

"And your first name?"

"Sergeant. Mr. Hodge, you're under arrest for vagrancy."

"Will I be given breakfast at the police station?"

"Sure."

After seventy-four years, I had my first ride in a police car. I was tempted to ask him to put on the siren. We rode in silence to the police station, arriving at just after 8:00 A.M. True to his word, Sergeant Rogers gave me a cup of coffee and jelly donut for breakfast while he filled out his arrest report.

"Mr. Hodge, I don't want to have to bring you to court. Who can come to pick you up?"

"Nobody, I'm afraid."

"How about your wife?"

"Deceased."

"Do you have any kids?"

"No."

"Friends or relatives?"

"No, sergeant. I am quite alone."

"I can't let you out of here so you can hitchhike to Florida. How about if I hook you up with somebody at social services. They might be able to find you temporary lodging, or room in a nursing home or something."

"I do not wish to live in a nursing home, officer. I have decided to move to Florida. I'm not aware of any law against that. In fact, I was under the impression that it was something of a requirement."

"Requirement? Look Mr. Hodge, if that's going to be your attitude, then I'm going to press charges for vagrancy. It's for your own good. Put on your coat, we're going to Westborough District Court."

"Excellent. That's on my way."

Sergeant Rogers insisted that I sit in the back of the car again for the fifteen minute ride to court. I had never even been called for jury duty before, so going to court was another first for me. I must say, I was enjoying my adventure immensely. Unfortunately, if I kept making such laggard progress, it was going to take me a month of Sundays to get to Florida.

We pulled up to the courthouse at ten minutes to nine. Sergeant Rogers brought me to a stenciled door that read, "Office of the Clerk For Criminal Business." My name was added to the list of people to be arraigned that morning.

"Good morning, Jake; how's business?" Sergeant Rogers asked the man behind the counter.

"Pretty good, Eddie. What brings you here today?"

"I want to add a vagrancy complaint to the list for this morning. I picked up this guy freezing his *cojones* off on Route 9 trying to hitchhike to Florida. He refuses any contact with social services. He may not take my suggestions, but I guess he'll listen to Judge Franklin."

I found it somewhat disconcerting that Sergeant Rogers, or Eddie as I now thought of him, would speak about me in my presence as if I was absent or unable to understand the conversation.

"Excuse me, Jake", I asked, "but what sort of criminal business do you conduct here?"

"What are you, a comedian?"

"No, sir. I am simply a man who both reads and speaks English. The sign on the door reads, "Office of The Clerk For Criminal Business." That implies that some sort of criminal business is conducted here, does it not?"

"It infers no such thing."

"I am aware of that. I made the inference due to the implication of the sign."

Jake turned away from me and back toward Eddie.

"I see what you mean, Eddie. Mr. Hodge is confused. He makes no sense."

"So, can you add him to Judge Franklin's docket?"

"Absolutely."

"Thanks. See you later."

Eddie took my arm and led me, as if I were blind, to a

courtroom. He whispered into the ear of a court officer. I was then seated in the prisoner dock with several other men and one woman. I was the only prisoner not handcuffed. Another first. I had never been a prisoner before. As each case was called, one of the other occupants in the dock would stand and face the judge. Judge Franklin sat in a high back leather chair. In front of him was a raised oak bench and behind him bookcases filled with green hardbound books containing the Massachusetts statutes and light brown hard bound books containing the reported Massachusetts case decisions. There were hundreds of books.

Judge Franklin himself was a short heavy man with curly gray hair. His black robe added to the effect of great girth. He peered myopically over half glasses that teetered near the end of his nose. The judge and courtroom clerk were very business-like and handled each case quickly and identically.

"Case No. 94 CR 5543, Commonwealth of Massachusetts v. Samuel Brown. Mr. Brown, please rise," intoned the clerk. The man to my left stood up. He was well dressed but appeared to be ill. He smelled of gin.

"Mr. Brown. You are charged with driving an automobile while intoxicated, failure to stop for a police officer, and driving to endanger. How do you plead?" asked the clerk.

"Not guilty," whispered Mr. Brown.

"Mr. Brown. If you are found guilty of the charges with which you face, you may be sentenced to the House of Correction. Therefore, you are entitled to an attorney. If you cannot afford an attorney, then one shall be appointed to represent you. Do you understand these rights, Mr. Brown?" asked Judge Franklin.

"Yes, sir. I mean, Your Honor."

"Very well. Do you wish to hire your own attorney, or would you like one appointed?"

"I'll hire my own lawyer, Your Honor."

"Very well. You will be released on your own recognizance. You must appear in court for a pre-trial conference on Wednesday, March twenty-third at 9:00 A.M. Don't forget, or a warrant will issue for your arrest. Stop by probation on your way out and you'll be given a notice with the date on it. That will be your only notice. Call the next case."

"Case No. 94 CR 5544, Commonwealth of Massachusetts v. George W. Hodge. Mr. Hodge, please rise."

I stood up in the dock and announced "Here I am, Your Honor." The police officers, clerk and Judge Franklin all laughed. The clerk sitting in front of the judge said to me, "Don't speak unless spoken to, Mr. Hodge. You are charged with vagrancy in violation of Massachusetts General Laws chapter 272 section 67. How do you plead?" asked the clerk.

"I don't know, sir."

"You must plead either guilty or not guilty. If you do not wish to make a plea, then a plea of not guilty shall be entered on your behalf. Do you wish to make a plea?"

"Yes, I do. But I need to know what vagrancy means in this court so I can make an intelligent choice. I found out from Jake this morning that, unfortunately, words sometime have meanings within a courthouse that they do not have elsewhere."

"Very well", said Judge Franklin. "Mr. Hodge has a right to be made aware of the charges against him." Judge Franklin then got up from his chair and pulled one of the green volumes from a shelf behind the bench. He sat down, adjusted his glasses and began to read aloud. "Massachusetts General Laws, chapter two hundred and seventy-two section sixty-seven states, in its entirety, "Sheriffs, deputy sheriffs, constables and police officers, acting on the request of any person or upon their own information or belief, shall without a warrant arrest and carry any vagrant before a district court for the purpose of

11

an examination, and shall make complaint against him."
Now, Mr. Hodge, how do you plead?"

"Your Honor, I do not wish to be bothersome, but I
still don't know. The statute you just read states that a
vagrant may be arrested and brought to court for
questioning, but it does not explain what a vagrant is.
Would you be so kind as to explain it to me?"

"Is the arresting officer here?"

Eddie separated himself from a group of uniformed
police officers and walked to the bench. "Yes, Your
Honor. Sergeant Edward Rogers, Shrewsbury Police."

"Gentlemen: For the purposes of the statute, a vagrant
is an idle person who, with no visible means of support,
lives without lawful employment, wanders abroad without
giving good account of himself, and places himself in
public places to beg and receive alms. Now, Sergeant
Rogers, what was Mr. Hodge doing when you arrested
him?"

"He was hitchhiking on Route 9 halfway into the right
lane in rush hour traffic."

"What is your address, Mr. Hodge?"

"I do not have one."

"Do you work, Mr. Hodge?"

"No, Your Honor. I am a retired English Professor."

"Where did you last work?"

"College of the Holy Cross."

"It sounds to me as if you would fit the description of a
vagrant, Mr. Hodge. Do you have anything to say?"

"I do, Your Honor. Having listened to the definition, I
am certain that I am not a vagrant, and I would choose to
plead not guilty. I do not have an address because I am
moving to Florida. I have never begged for or received
alms, Your Honor. Last night, I slept in a hotel, and I
suppose I could do the same tonight. I have eight hundred
dollars in my possession, so I do have a visible means of
support."

"Do you have a place to stay in Florida, or somebody

to stay with, Mr. Hodge?"

"Not yet, Your Honor. I only decided to move two days ago when my house was sold. Is lack of planning a crime, Your Honor?"

"No, Mr. Hodge, it is not. But if you just sold your house and have cash, why don't you buy a plane, train or bus ticket to Florida?"

"I am trying to save the little money that I have, Your Honor. I am not required by law to travel by public transportation, am I?"

"No, Mr. Hodge. There are laws against hitchhiking however, in this and most other states. I suggest you change your plans or find an alternate means of transportation. I'm going to dismiss this case, Mr. Hodge, but I urge you to talk to someone here in probation. They can connect you with social services. Somebody there may be able to help you."

"Thank you, Your Honor. However, if it is all right, I would rather help myself. This has been my first time in court, and I must say I have enjoyed the experience. Thank you for your kindness and wisdom, Your Honor, but if it is all right with you, I will be leaving now."

"It is not all right with me, but you are free to go. Please be careful, Mr. Hodge."

"Thank you."

As I walked toward the door of the courtroom, Sergeant Rogers stopped me.

"Mr. Hodge, may I have a moment of your time?"

"Certainly, Eddie. What can I do for you?"

"Mr. Hodge, you seem like a nice guy. I don't know why you decided to thumb it down to Florida, but you must have better options. You said you just sold your house. You must have some money from that."

"No, Eddie. I said my house was just sold. It was a foreclosure auction. I did not get any money from the sale."

"Eight hundred bucks isn't going to last you very long.

13

Why don't you let me take you over to social services? You know it's a better option."

"It may be a safer option, but I do not believe that it's a better option. I've had a wonderful life here. I raised a family and loved my work. Now, through circumstances which I do not wish to explain, I find myself in quite a fix. I do not wish to add sad and bitter memories to the cherished memories of a lifetime well spent. I'm going to Florida to live out my life in a new place where the weather is warm. Thank you for your concern, Eddie, but I have made up my mind." Eddie and I shook hands and went our separate ways.

I must admit, I was not particularly anxious to go back outside into the cold, so I returned to the courtroom to watch Judge Franklin work. He had finished the arraignments while I was speaking to Eddie, so I sat down on a bench to collect my thoughts.

"First call of the list for 209A Protection from Abuse Cases. First case on the list, 94-5352, Ann Marie Fobbs v. Christian R. Lovett," announced the clerk. "Will all parties and witnesses please approach the bench."

A stunning young woman stood up from the spectator section and walked to the judge. She was holding the hand of a young girl. It was obvious that they were mother and daughter. Both had the same olive complexion and long, thick black hair. A man also stood up and walked to the bench. He was a nice looking young man with blond hair and a cleft in his chin. The clerk asked both parties to raise their right hands. Both the man and woman raised their right hand. The little girl looked confused but raised her right hand so as not to offend anyone.

"Do you swear to tell the truth, the whole truth, and nothing but the truth, so help you God?" asked the clerk.

"I do," said the man and woman in unison. "Me too," added the girl.

Judge Franklin took over the proceedings. "This is a return on a Massachusetts General Laws chapter 209A petition for protection from abuse. An ex parte order was made last Friday prohibiting Mr. Lovett from going within one hundred yards of Ms. Fobbs or her daughter or their residence; from calling or contacting them in any way; or from threatening or abusing Ms. Fobbs. In addition, Mr. Lovett was ordered out of the parties' home at 34 Glendale Road in Shrewsbury. Those orders expire today and these proceedings are to determine whether the order shall be extended for one year. Ms. Fobbs, I will hear from you first."

"What do you want to know, judge?"

"Do you believe that you will be in imminent danger of physical harm from Mr. Lovett if the order is not extended?"

"I believe that he'll kill me, or at least beat me up again, judge."

"Has Mr. Lovett ever struck you, Ms. Fobbs?"

"You bet, Your Honor; look at this!" Miss Fobbs lifted her shirt up to expose several large purple bruises over her ribs.

"All right. Please lower your shirt, Ms. Fobbs. Mr. Lovett, what do you have to say?"

"Judge, it's over between us. I never laid a hand on her except to try to push her away from me when she started swinging at me. I don't care if the order is extended for a year except for one thing: I need her out of *my* house."

"Do you own the house together with Ms. Fobbs?"

"No, judge, I owned that house from before I even met her. I'm a carpenter, judge, and my shop and business phone are at the house. So are all my tools. I can't earn a living if I can't go back."

"I notice that Ms. Fobbs is not seeking any child support. Is this girl your daughter, Mr. Lovett?"

"No way, judge."

"Ms. Fobbs, do you have anything to add?"

"Yes. I've been working for this man for the past year." Somehow, she made the word "man" sound like the vilest of insults. "As of now, I guess I've got no job and no place to live. If you kick us out, me and Bobbi will be living out of my truck."

"Where you are not married to Mr. Lovett, and the girl is not Mr. Lovett's daughter, I'm afraid that I cannot deprive him of his house, which he owned before meeting you. I will continue the stay away order for one year. Mr. Lovett may move back into his house at 3:00 this afternoon. By that time, you will have to remove your belongings from the house. A copy of this order will be forwarded to the Shrewsbury Police Department today for enforcement. At such time as you establish another residence, Ms. Fobbs, please alert the court, and a copy of the restraining order will be sent to that police department as well. Please call the next case, Mr. Clerk."

I did not realize that such dreary and depressing details of people's lives were the typical fodder for the courts. I put on my coat, picked up my valise and left the court to begin walking through Westborough to Route 9 to continue my trip. I was perhaps a quarter mile from the courthouse when a green pick-up truck skidded to a stop next to me. The passenger side door flew open and Miss Fobbs and her daughter were inside.

"Get in, professor; it's cold out, and I've got a proposition for you."

"I really must be on my way, Miss. I do not plan on being in this area so..."

"Yeah, yeah, I know. You're going to Florida. I heard the whole vagrancy thing when I was waiting my turn. Just get in and shut the door and listen. It's colder than hell out there. Throw your bag in the back."

I put my suitcase on the bed of the truck and climbed inside the cab. Miss Fobbs jerked the truck into gear and we lurched forward. I fumbled for the seat belt while her daughter giggled.

Miss Fobbs got right down to business. "I heard your story in front of the judge today. I think you heard mine, too. You're going to Florida, and someplace warm sounds pretty good to me right now. I'm not going to stick around here and wait for that..." She hesitated and cast a sidelong glance at her daughter, "...man to kill me. So here's my proposition: you share the driving and split the gas, and you can come with me and Bobbi. It beats hitchhiking. What do you say?"

"Under the circumstances, Miss Fobbs, that is quite agreeable to me. As we have not been properly introduced, please allow me to introduce myself. My name is George Hodge."

"Pleased to meet you, GW. I'm Ann Marie, and this is my babygirl, Bobbi. Bobbi, say hi to GW."

"Hi, GW."

"Hello, Bobbi. Is that short for Roberta?"

"Yeah, but nobody ever calls me that."

"May I call you Roberta then? It's a lovely name."

The girl mumbled, "Bobbi, Roberta, Bobbi, Roberta, Bobbi, Roberta," and paused. "Yes. Roberta sounds more grown up, so you may call me Roberta."

"Thank you, Roberta," I answered. She smiled.

2. Heading South

*A*nn Marie drove us to her now ex-boyfriend's house to remove her belongings as well as her daughter's. She purchased a cup of coffee at a Dunkin Donuts drive through and then proceeded to navigate the winding country roads at what I considered to be an imprudent speed, all the while with one hand on the wheel and the other on her coffee cup. She kept up a steady stream of conversation with Roberta and occasionally switched the coffee cup to her left hand and wiped jelly off Roberta's face with her right. During those interludes she would steer the truck with her knees. As I was still somewhat unsure of my standing with Ann Marie, I remained silent and listened to the beating of my heart against my chest.

We pulled into a gravel driveway by a wooden sign that read, "Christian Lovett Carpentry." The long driveway sloped down a hill to a large wooden house that I can only describe as a rather rustic looking affair with stained barn board siding. The house was on a wooded lot and set back quite a distance from a sparsely populated road. Next to the house stood a barn approximately one and one half times larger than the house. The barn housed Mr. Lovett's shop and carpentry office. The door was closed and locked with a large padlock.

Ann Marie stepped down from the truck and pulled out Roberta after her.

"Come on in with me, GW; it's too cold to wait out here."

I gingerly stepped out of the truck and followed Ann Marie and Roberta into the house.

Ann Marie instructed Roberta, "I've got to pack us up, Bobbigirl, so why don't you take GW into the other room and watch TV? I think *Shining Time Station* is on."

"Okay, Mommy. Come on, GW; we can watch TV."

I followed Roberta into the living room. She rummaged through the couch cushions until she found two remote controls. Roberta sat on a couch facing the television and asked me to sit next to her. She then turned on the television with one remote and found the station she wanted while she used a second remote to adjust the volume.

"This is my show! You can sit here, but don't touch the clickers" she warned.

We watched the station master, Staci Jones, outsmart a greedy ill-dressed man named Schemer. I could not determine his position other than as a train station employee. I suppose it was not bad as television goes. I actually enjoyed the musical number, "Fifteen Miles Down the Erie Canal," performed by puppets in an old-style juke box.

We were interrupted by Ann Marie calling to me from a bedroom upstairs. I ascended the stairs. At the top were a steamer trunk and a wooden toy chest. The steamer trunk looked to be from the time of my youth. I was a bit surprised that Ann Marie had such a relic.

"These are most of our worldly possessions, GW. Will

you help me carry them out to the truck?"

"I will try, Ann Marie, but I fear that I am not as strong as I once was."

"Just grab an end, professor; I need a hand, not an excuse."

Ann Marie led the way down the stairs, so she carried the heavier end. We stopped once on the way down so I could rest. When I put down my end, Ann Marie braced the trunk to keep it from sliding down the stairs. After a moment, I told her I was ready to continue.

"Wait a minute, GW. There's no reason to make this tougher than it's got to be." She then moved aside and allowed the trunk to slide down the stairs. It hit the wall at the foot of the stairs with a plaster-cracking smash.

"I don't give a rat's ass about this place anymore. Let the carpenter fix the wall. Come on, let's carry it out to my truck."

We put the trunk in the truck and went back for the toy chest. The toy chest was filled with dolls, balls, blocks and the odds and ends of childhood. The chest itself was a light pine decorated with a circus parade painted around the sides. On the top, two painted clowns held a banner which said "Bobbi Fobbs." The chest shone with a coat of protective varnish.

"We have to be more careful with this, GW; it's Bobbigirl's pride and joy."

"I can see why; it is a lovely chest. Custom made?"

"You bet! It took me forever to finish it. The carpentry's a cinch, but the painting was a bitch."

"You did a marvelous job. You're quite a talented artist."

"Thanks. Just be careful with this; it isn't nearly as heavy as the trunk."

We carried the chest out to the truck. Ann Marie opened the lock to the barn and went inside. She emerged a few minutes later with a heavy tarpaulin and some rope to cover our belongings. After tying down the load, Ann

Marie collected Roberta and we climbed into the cab. When we were halfway up the driveway, a panel truck pulled across the mouth of the driveway to block the exit to the street. The side of the truck had a hand-painted sign designed to look like the wood sign hanging by the driveway. It too read "Christian Lovett Carpentry."

Mr. Lovett jumped out of his truck and walked over to the driver's side where Ann Marie sat.

"You aren't supposed to be near me and you aren't supposed to be here until three o'clock. Beat it, before I call the cops. They'll throw you in jail for violating a restraining order."

"Well, you aren't supposed to be ripping me off either. That's my tarp on the truck. And what's underneath it? Probably my tools..."

"I didn't take any of your tools, just *my* tool box. You can take the cost of the tarp out of the two weeks wages you still owe me. Now get out of the way."

"I'm not moving until I take the tarp off the truck."

Ann Marie said, "Wrong again." She threw the truck into reverse and backed down the driveway toward the house. Mr. Lovett walked to the top of the driveway to his panel truck. He opened the sliding door facing us and removed a crowbar. He slapped the crowbar into the palm of his left hand and began to walk toward us. Ann Marie pushed the gear shift to drive and pressed the accelerator to the floor. I could hear gravel being dislodged underneath the tires and knocked against the wheel wells. Mr. Lovett dropped the crowbar and put up his hands as if he would stop the truck bearing down. Ann Marie never let up on the accelerator. Mr. Lovett tried to jump out of the way, but his left ankle was clipped by the bumper. We were still accelerating when our truck hit the open door of the panel truck. The impact pushed the panel truck several feet back from the driveway. Ann Marie backed up her truck past the prostrate form of Christian Lovett and then sped forward and rammed the van again. That pushed it back far enough into the street so she could leave the driveway. As we drove away, Christian Lovett was sitting up and screaming. Through Ann Marie's open window I could hear Lovett's threats.

"I'll get you and your fucking brat, you bitch!"

Bobbi laughed with delight. "That was fun, Mommy!"

"Why don't you take a nap now, Bobbigirl. We have a long ride ahead of us."

"Okay, Mommy," she said. Young Roberta leaned against my shoulder and closed her eyes. I had forgotten how quickly children can travel from action to sleep, and within minutes I heard the regular, untroubled breathing of the little girl.

Roberta slept quietly while Ann Marie drove east on Route 9 through Shrewsbury and Westborough. The sides of the road were filled by one strip mall after another with an occasional free-standing building or apartment complex. When I was a boy in Worcester, that same stretch of road was mostly forest and farmland. We picked up Interstate Route 495 in Westborough and joined the lines of cars, trucks and buses speeding along at seventy miles per hour. We reached the Interstate Route 95 exchange in Mansfield. According to our map, Route 95 was a straight stretch of highway tracing the Atlantic coast from Maine to south Florida.

Within fifteen minutes we crossed our first state line together and entered Rhode Island. "The Biggest Little State In The Union," bragged the road sign. Almost as soon as we crossed into Rhode Island Ann Marie loosened her grip on the wheel and leaned back a bit more in her seat. She crossed from the passing lane to the right lane.

"Are you in a hurry, GW?" she asked me.

"A hurry to do what?"

"To get where we're going."

"Not at all, Ann Marie."

"Good. Then we're taking the scenic route."

At the next interchange Ann Marie turned off the highway onto Route 1, the old coastal route from Maine to Florida. She pulled into the parking lot of a convenience store and got out of the truck. As she stretched her arms and legs in the parking lot, men and women stared at her. She is a magnificent looking woman. Ann Marie then opened my door and got inside.

"I got us out of Massachusetts, GW. Now it's your turn to drive. Slide over. I got some sleep to catch up on."

I moved over, trying not to wake Roberta.

"Don't worry about her, GW; she can sleep through anything."

As if to prove that, Ann Marie lifted her daughter's head up and then put her back on her lap. Roberta let out a few grunts of protest, but never opened her eyes. Within minutes both mother and daughter were asleep. I proceeded south on Route One. I had never driven a vehicle that large before and it took several miles to get used to looking down on traffic from high in the cab. I was also a bit out of practice driving, but Ann Marie and Roberta slept soundly through my occasional herky-jerky stops and starts.

The road wound south through Pawtucket and Providence. It was lined by strip malls, fast food stores and garish electric signs. South of Providence the scenery was a bit more rural and I could even smell a hint of the ocean somewhere off to the east. By the time I made Connecticut, both Roberta and Ann Marie had awakened. There was a light snow beginning to fall and it was mucking up the windshield. I was looking to the left of the dashboard trying to find the windshield wiper switch when I heard the tremendous honk from the horn of a large tractor trailer. While looking for the windshield wipers, I fear I neglected the road and drifted into the northbound lane. I looked up to see the windshield filled with truck.

Apparently Ann Marie looked up at the same instant, because as I pulled the wheel hard to the right, I heard her scream. I overcompensated and two wheels went off the shoulder on the right. I was able to bring the truck under control without hitting anybody or anything.

"That was fun, GW! Can we do that again?" Roberta asked.

"Forget it, Bobbigirl," Ann Marie answered on my behalf. "Why don't you pull over at the next place with a bathroom, GW? I'm sure that Bobbigirl has to pee. Besides, I think I'd feel safer if I were driving."

I pulled into a gas station in Mystic, Connecticut. After taking care of nature's call, Ann Marie took the wheel. She drove to the scenic village on the water and stopped. She grabbed Roberta's hand and began to pull her out of the truck. "You coming, GW?"

"Of course," I answered. I had nowhere else to go after all.

The temperature was no more than ten or fifteen degrees, but there was no wind and the snow had stopped. Stars shone in the sky. The noise of clattering cutlery and laughing couples floated from the restaurants near the pier. Ann Marie walked to a bench on the pier and sat down with Roberta.

"Can you find the north star, Roberta?"

"Yes, Mommy, there it is, past the handle of the Big Dipper."

"That's right. You can always count on the stars, Bobbigirl. We're going far away. The trees will look different and the weather will be different. Even the people will talk with a funny accent. But if you look up at the Florida sky every night, do you know what you'll see? The same stars, in the very same place. The same Big Dipper, Little Dipper, North star, Orion's Belt, and all the rest. You remember that, Bobbigirl."

"Mommy, I'm hungry. Can we eat at that restaurant? The one that looks like a boat?"

"I don't think so, honey—too expensive. Besides, you only eat hamburgers, anyway. How about we find a

Wendy's or a McDonald's?"

"Yes! Let's do that!"

"Okay. I want to take a little walk to stretch my legs, and then we can go back to the truck."

3. The Unwanted Child

*W*e continued south on Route One through Groton and New London to South Lyme, where we stopped at a Burger King. We ordered three children's meals and sat down at a small plastic table and unwrapped the packaging that was keeping our hamburgers warm. Is it my imagination, or are hamburgers more bland today than they were in my youth? In any event, I would not have been able to enjoy a proper meal as Roberta decided it was time to ask me questions.

"How old are you, GW?" she asked.

"I am seventy-four years old. How old are you Roberta?"

"I'm asking the questions, GW! You have to wait your turn, Okay?"

"Okay" I assured her, only slightly chastened.

"Are you married?"

"Not anymore. My wife passed on."

"Passed on what?"

"Passed on living."

"You mean she died, right?"

"Right."

"Well, why didn't you just say so? You talk funny, GW."

"Young lady, I hereby pledge that I shall endeavor to speak to you in a plain and simple manner. Would that please you?"

"What?"

"I'll keep it simple."

"Good. How come you call me Roberta? Everybody else calls me Bobbi, you know."

"Do you want me to call you Bobbi?"

"No, I like it when you call me Roberta. But just you, okay?"

"Okay, Roberta."

Roberta shook her head seriously as though we had just reached a decision of lasting importance. Then she turned her attention to her French fried potatoes.

Ann Marie and I decided we should try to make New York before finding a place to stay for the night.

"I'll feel better when I get out of New England. I don't trust that sonofabitch Lovett."

Ann Marie drove along Route One into New Haven and then picked up Route 34 which runs west along the Housatonic River. Neither of us wanted to drive through or spend the night in New York City, so we had to go around it. While she drove I spread the map over the laps of Roberta and myself and tried to read the nearly indecipherable print by the meager illumination coming from the dome light in the cab. The rural countryside provided a darker night than I am used to, having spent so many years in a city. Roberta helped spot the street signs that led us to Newtown and then Danbury, Connecticut. Suddenly we were in Mill Plain, New York, wriggling free of the weight of our past.

The Putnam Motel provided cheap rates and a

continental breakfast of coffee from the pot in the lobby by the front desk and a day-old pastry encased in cellophane wrap. To save money we shared one room. Ann Marie and Roberta shared one bed and I had the other. We were all tired and decided to forego television and turn in.

"I need a bedtime story, Mommy."

"Okay, Bobbigirl. What story do you want to hear tonight?"

"I want GW to tell me a story."

Ann Marie glanced over to me to determine whether I would be agreeable to telling a story. I nodded my assent and Roberta lay down with the covers pulled up to her chin. I cleared my throat and dusted off the story telling voice I had put into storage decades ago.

"Once upon a time, long, long ago, in a land far, far away, lived a little girl named Belle. Belle lived with her beautiful loving mother, named Portia, and her step father, Lear. Lear was a handsome man who seemed nice at first. He was fun to be around, and could tell a good joke.

"After a while, Lear began to change. First it was little things. His jokes became more mean than funny. He began to order Belle and Portia to do chores while he relaxed and drank grog. Finally, he began to hit Portia. When Portia said she would leave, he threatened to hurt her and Belle.

"Portia was sad and didn't know what to do. Belle wanted to help, so she visited her friend, Shelly. Shelly was a wise old turtle that lived in the pond behind Belle's home. Shelly could remember back to a time before the little cottage where Belle lived was built and before people came to the countryside. In her long years, Shelly watched, and she listened, and she learned.

"Shelly, I need your help," said little Belle. "My

28

stepfather, Lear, is very mean to mother and me. I'm afraid that one day he will hurt mother."

"What does Lear give you?" asked Shelly.

"He gives me a warm house to live in and food to eat," answered Belle.

"What does Lear take?" asked Shelly.

"He takes nothing from me," answered Belle.

"Shelly shook her head and stared at Belle. "Oh, but he takes what is most valuable from you. Are you happy, Belle?" asked Shelly.

"No," said Belle.

"Is your mother happy? Does she still laugh and sing the way she used to?"

"Not anymore," said Belle sadly. "Since we came to live with Lear we are not happy."

"Where did your happiness go?"

"I don't know, Shelly."

"What is it you would rather have, your splendid house with Lear, or the happiness your mother and you have lost?" asked Shelly.

"I would rather have our happiness."

"Lear has taken your happiness away" said Shelly. "You must follow your heart and leave Lear."

"You mean run away?" asked Belle.

"No. You mustn't run away from Lear. You must chase your happiness. Do not stop until you reach it."

"Where shall we go?"

"You must find that for yourself, Belle," said Shelly. Then she slid off the bank and beneath the surface of the pond, leaving only ripples to prove she had been there at all. Belle ran home to tell her mother what Shelly had said. Portia thought for a moment and then knelt down in front of Belle and held her daughter's shoulders.

"Belle, if we leave here, what shall we eat?

Where shall we go? How shall we stay warm at night?"

"We can follow the stars, Mother. As long as we see the same stars in the sky, we'll always be home."

"Portia considered what Bell had said, and decided that Belle was right. That night when Lear was asleep, Portia and Belle collected all their belongings and put them in a cart and left Lear forever. Wherever they went, they had each other. And they found happiness together under the stars."

"Good-night now, Roberta, sleep tight," I said. And then I got a treat I had not had in thirty years. I got a hug and a kiss good-night from a sweet little girl. Ann Marie and I stepped outside of the room for a few minutes to let Roberta fall asleep.

"That was a real subtle story, GW. What about you? What's your story?"

I thought a moment, and then quoted Shakespeare for Ann Marie:

> "How heavy do I journey on the way,
> When what I seek, my weary travel's end,
> Doth teach that ease and that repose to say,
> "Thus far the miles are measured from thy friend!"
> The beast that bears me, tired with my woe,
> Plods dully on, to bear that weight in me,
> As if by some instinct the wretch did know
> His rider loved no speed being made from thee.
> For that same groan doth put this in my mind:
> My grief lies onward and my joy behind."

"Well, you sure are one depressing old fart, GW. Hell, I hope this ride gets better for you."

"Ann Marie, I could not be happier with the ride up to

this point. I am truly enjoying the splendid company of both you and Roberta. I still catch myself thinking about how I will describe the day to Kat."

"Well, good. Let's call it a night."

I awoke the next morning and showered and shaved before Ann Marie or Roberta stirred. Then I left the room to purchase a newspaper and bring back coffee for Ann Marie and myself. This was to become the morning routine for our journey. The girls awoke soon after I returned to the room, and I watched the news while they prepared themselves to face the day. We purchased a hearty breakfast at a diner next to the motel and then spread out our maps to plan that day's adventure on the road. Our goal was to make Virginia.

We checked out of the motel and continued west on Route 6. The town of Mahopac was so pretty and rustic that it was hard to believe we were within a few hours of New York City. The road wound around Lake Mahopac through the Hudson River Valley until we crossed the Hudson River into Harriman. It was the first of three major rivers we planned to cross that day.

We rolled over the hills through towns with names like Monroe and Goshen. The trees were bare except for the occasional stubborn brown and withered leaf that refused to let go of a branch. Pine trees added an occasional bit of green under the coating of rime. The road was stained white by the salt used throughout the winter. We caught route 284 in Slate Hill, New York, and soon crossed into Sussex, New Jersey. Another state line crossed, another excuse for a rest.

We spilled out of the truck into the parking lot of a Denny's. Ann Marie knew that Roberta had been building up energy while cooped up in the cab. That energy had to be dissipated, I was told, or Roberta was liable to launch into sustained screaming, punching and crying.

"Hey, Bobbigirl, I bet I can beat you in a race," Ann

Marie challenged Roberta.

"No way, Mommy."

"Yes, I can; let's race."

"I don't want to race; I want to go pee-pee."

"You can race me first. Nobody has an accident during a race," Ann Marie assured her daughter.

"I don't know, Mommy; it's cold out, you know."

"Okay. If you're a big worm-eating chicken whose afraid, then you don't have to race me."

"I am not a chicken!"

"Then race me five times around the Denny's."

Roberta's answer was the bobbing of her hood as she ran toward the far end of the restaurant. Ann Marie loped off after her. I went inside to get a table by the window. I waved to Roberta and she smiled at me each lap. When I was drinking my second cup of coffee I realized they had passed me seven times. Apparently the length of the race was growing. I suspected that Roberta's counting skills were not up to the task of keeping track of the laps. Finally, Ann Marie and Roberta joined me, both red-faced and short of breath.

"That was fun, GW! You should have run with us," Roberta informed me.

"I insist on pacing myself for the long haul, Roberta. I noticed that you won the race."

"I always win. Mommy's a slow poke."

"I could tell."

I rather enjoyed the macaroni and cheese lunch with a bottomless cup of coffee. Roberta and Ann Marie split a meal from the children's menu. When the check came I made sure that I paid for most of the bill. Ann Marie's lack of a good meal was more likely the result of a shortage of cash than appetite. After lunch I took the wheel, filled up the tank, and we were off.

I proceded south through Pellettown and Andover when I heard the soft rhythmic sleeping of Roberta. Ann Marie decided it was time to pick up the slack in conversation. She was more chatty when acting as navigator than she had been as pilot.

"So, what's your story, GW? Are you going to live with your kids or something?"

"I don't have any children any more, Ann Marie. My son and daughter are both gone."

"I usually wouldn't pry, but hell, it's a long ride. May I ask what happened?"

"Yes, you may," I answered. Then I took a deep breath and started near the beginning.

"I had two children, a son, Michael, and daughter, Jennifer. They were both older than you. Michael was born on May 2, 1947, and Jenny was born on August 14, 1950. Michael was a hellion almost as soon as he was born. He managed to climb out of his crib when he was only nine months old; after that, there was no catching him.

"You should have seen him; he was beautiful. He grew to be tall, like me, but that was where the resemblance ended. He had thick, dark, curly hair and startling green eyes. In high school, he played every sport in its season. He excelled without practice or effort. If he had actually worked at it, he may have been a successful athlete, but sports were never more than a hobby or diversion.

"School never seemed to interest him much either. He attended his classes and generally brought home Bs with an occasional C. I do not recall that he ever brought a book home with him. When I questioned him about homework, Michael always assured me that he did it in study hall. If Michael suffered from any curse, it was that everything came too easily to him. He was popular and successful in school without effort. Michael thought he was invincible."

"So, what happened to him?" Ann Marie asked.

"Michael never bothered to apply to a College. He decided to kick around the country for a few years after high school and then decide what he wanted to do. Michael worked that summer to save enough money to start his journey in the autumn. He was drafted in October 1965, four months after graduating from high school and exactly two weeks after leaving home to see the world. I begged him to go to Holy Cross. As a professor, I could have gotten him enrolled immediately so he would be eligible for a student deferment. He refused the offer.

"What are you worried about, Dad? I'll probably never have to go overseas, and even if I do, I'll be careful. You made it through World War Two; don't you think I can last a year in Vietnam if I have to?"

"The question broke my heart. I did not realize how innocent Michael was. I did survive three years in the North African and European theaters in the Second World War. I saw very few men killed or injured because they were careless. When a mortar shell explodes next to you, or you step on a land mine, it does not matter how careful you are. When your company is ordered to advance against a machine gun emplacement, it does not matter how careful you are. I am afraid that war does not discriminate. Shrapnel does not spare the strong and kill the weak.

"I saw horrors in those years that are so ingrained in my mind, that occasionally I have nightmares that are exact replays of events I witnessed. The nightmares have the absolute clarity of a waking experience. I can see the bright sun of the desert illuminate every grain of sand in my vision. I can smell the cordite from fired rounds. I hear the thumping sound of the cannon on tanks that is strangely muted by the vast space of the desert. I even feel the wetness of blood and viscera splattered on me coming from Private Stanley Ozer after he was struck in the belly by a shell.

"I had eighteen years to tell that to Michael. I could have taught him the ultimate horror of war. For foot soldiers, survival is based almost entirely on luck. Are you lucky enough to have competent officers? Will the sniper taking aim at you miss? Will your weapon misfire when you need it the most?"

I then told Ann Marie something I had never told anyone, not even Katherine. "One morning in Italy, my company was ordered to move to a location to the west. We were nearing our targeted position when I tripped and fell over my own feet. I had probably marched more than one thousand miles during the previous two and a half years without so much as a stumble. On that sunny day, on a flat smooth road, I fell. As I fell, a bullet passed over me and stuck the man behind me in the chest.

"We all dove for cover. A medic in our company ran to the man that was shot. The medic was shot in the head. Falling down saved my life. But it cost the lives of two other men. Of the hundreds of lifeless bodies I saw, theirs are the two faces that haunt me most. Michael did not understand that his grace and strength would mean little in the cauldron of battle. If I had told that story to Michael, and others like it, perhaps he would not have been so cavalier in his attitude toward joining the army.

"Michael shipped out to boot camp just after Thanksgiving of 1965. Four weeks later he was in a Jeep that flipped over. His neck was broken and he died instantly. For me, Michael is frozen at nineteen years old. I see him as that beautiful boy on the threshold of manhood, neither child nor man."

After a few minutes of silence I turned to Ann Marie and said, "That is what became of my son".

During my story about Michael we had left Route 284 and turned onto New Jersey Route 40 in Buena. We soon were forced onto our first major highway of the day, the New Jersey Turnpike in Deepwater. After a short while we crossed our second major river of the day, the Delaware, and into the state of Delaware—our fifth state since starting the trip. As I finished telling Ann Marie about Michael, we were leaving Delaware Route 9 and catching Route 8 near Pearson's Corner. It was time to switch drivers.

Roberta awoke as I opened the door. She got out of the truck and asked if we could take a walk. The February air was warmed a bit by the Chesapeake Bay and did not have the malevolent bite that it had had in Worcester. Was it only yesterday that I'd begun this journey? Ann Marie locked the truck and we walked along the main street in Pearson's Corner. Roberta looked in store windows and admired some of the wares for sale, but never asked her mother to buy her anything.

There was a small town green with a bandstand in the town center. Roberta climbed up on the bandstand and gave an impromptu concert. After singing and dancing through "Waddle De Acha," "America the Beautiful" and a few others, we started back to the truck. I had my hands in my pockets and my head down when Ann Marie yelled to me, "Watch out for Bobbi!" and she began to sprint down the street.

I looked up to see Ann Marie bearing down on two teenage boys who were trying to pull the toy chest off of the back of the truck. Ann Marie never yelled at them to stop or warned them of her approach. She ran right into one of the boys without seeming to slow down. She hit him in the small of the back with her knee and behind the neck with her right forearm. The boy slammed into the tailgate and collapsed in a heap.

I glanced down at Roberta, who seemed entirely unconcerned. I suggested that we speed up to help her mother.

"Forget it, GW; that will only make her mad."

Nevertheless, I held onto Roberta's hand and broke into a trot. As I approached, the second boy swung a wild haymaker at Ann Marie. She leaned back so his fist went by her face. As she did so, she put her hand by his fist and seemed to effortlessly guide his hand behind his back with her right hand. She grabbed his hair with her left hand and then stomped down hard with her right foot behind the boy's right knee.

When I reached the truck, both boys were lying on the ground curled up and crying. Both of the boys, about sixteen years old I would guess, were a good deal bigger than Ann Marie. I had no doubt that either one of them could make short work of me. Roberta pulled the wallets out of their back pockets and told them she was going to turn them over to the police. We got into the truck and drove away.

We picked up Route 44 to Route 300 and then west on State 213. When we were on Route 301 and heading toward the Potomac River, Ann Marie pulled over at an Arby's in Chester. She took the money out of the wallets and threw the wallets in the trash.

"Well, GW, looks like I just got myself an extra forty-two dollars," she told me.

"Ann Marie, where did you learn how to do that?"

"When I was a dancer at Club Jiggles in Worcester, I dated one of the bouncers. He taught me a few moves to defend myself."

"You were a stripper?"

"An exotic dancer, GW. And why do you look so surprised? Don't you think I'm good looking enough? You don't think that men would pay to see me dance naked?"

When she asked me that, I experienced a sensation I had not felt in years. I was blushing. As I felt the heat rise in my face I answered with all the dignity I could muster, "Ann Marie, we both know that you are extremely attractive. I was only surprised because that is not a profession that seems to suit your personality."

"That's why I gave it up. But you know what, GW? That was the best paying job I ever had. On a Friday or Saturday night I could clear four hundred dollars. Mostly tips, so it was all under the table. It wasn't easy walking away from a gig like that."

"Mommy?"

"Yes Babygirl?"

"Will you teach me how to fight like that?"

"Later, honey. After we get to Florida."

"Okay."

"What did you do after working as an exotic dancer?" I asked.

"Lots of things. I'm a damn good carpenter. I've done everything from framing to finish work. I've done some clerical and receptionist work too, but I hated that. And I've waitressed and been a short order cook. I was good at every single job I ever had, but no matter how good I am with a hammer, typewriter or spatula, the only decent money I ever made was shaking my tits."

"I, on the other hand, have held only two paying jobs in my entire life. My first job was as a soldier in the United States Army, and the second was College English Professor. I do not believe that anybody would have ever paid to see me shake anything attached to my body."

Ann Marie laughed and suggested that we move on to Virginia, pointing out that the boys she beat up might report that they were robbed, and that it might be a good idea for us to cross the State line. We all climbed back into the truck and continued along Delaware Route 301. We reached the Chesapeake Bay Bridge and crossed the Chesapeake Bay. Roberta was wonderstruck, claiming that it must be the biggest bridge on earth.

It was getting dark as we swung south through Upper Marlboro, Rosaryville, and Mattawoman. Finally, we reached the Governor Nice Memorial Bridge and crossed our third major river of the day, the Potomac. Having made Virginia, we decided to find a place to spend the night. We chose the King George Motor Court in Edgeville. We ate at a local diner called the Trainwreck. It was an old fashioned diner shaped like the car of a train. Roberta could not have been more impressed by dinner at the Ritz.

"Mommy, this restaurant looks like a train! Will it move while we eat?"

"No, Bobbigirl. The diner only looks like a train. It isn't

real. It isn't on tracks either. It's in a parking lot."

"Well, I like it. I'm going to pretend that the train is taking us far away. Where do you want the train to go, GW?"

"I would like to ride to Casablanca on the Orient Express," I answered.

"Well, forget it, GW. We are going to the moon!"

While we ate the meatloaf with brown gravy, mashed potatoes and green peas, Roberta would occasionally look out the window and describe the sights.

"Look, a meteor!" or "Watch out for that space ship!" All in all, it was a rather pleasant meal. After dinner we returned to the motor court. After an hour or so of television, it was time for Roberta to go to bed.

"I want GW to tell me another story before I go to bed, Mommy!" pleaded Roberta.

"That's up to GW, Bobbigirl. You ask him yourself, and see what he says."

"GW?"

"Yes, Roberta?"

"Would you tell me a story?"

"I would be delighted. What kind of a story would you like tonight?"

"Something with monsters."

"I know just the story. It is about a circus family named the Swinging Swangos. The Swango family had a mother named Doris, a father named Bill, and three girls named Bobbin, Robin, and Dobbin. The whole family was in a trapeze act and all five of them would swing through the air together. They would do flips, and somersaults and spins. And just when it seemed as if one of the Swangos would fall to the floor of the circus tent, another would swing over and catch her.

"One day, the circus train was traveling from Sharpsville to the town of Holy Oak for the next show. All of a sudden, the wheels of the train screeched to a halt. The train stopped so hard that people fell everywhere. The bearded lady fell on top of the sword swallower. Lawrence the Lion Tamer bumped into Crenshaw the Clown; who fell against a huge red ball used in the elephant act; that rolled into Bobbin Swango; who fell right out of the train!

"Bobbin looked ahead to see why the train had stopped, and do you know what she saw? Sitting on the tracks was the biggest dragon anybody had ever seen. It was as tall as a pine tree and as wide as five cows. He had thick green scaly skin that was as hard as armor. The dragon's teeth and claws were shiny and black and as sharp as razors. Fire came out of his mouth and nose when he spoke. And when he spread his wings, they were so wide that the entire valley was cast in shadow.

"Bobbin was angry that the dragon had stopped the train, so she walked up to the dragon and climbed right up his tail, across his back, over his head, and onto his snout. She turned to face him and said, "What do you think you're doing? We have a show to do in Holy Oak. Get off this track right now!"

"The dragon looked at Bobbin and plucked her off his nose. Then the dragon gave a tremendous laugh that shook the entire train. "Nobody tells me what to do in my valley! And nobody may pass unless they are able to defeat me. Who among you dares to face Rupert The Dragon?" he bellowed.

"My family and I can beat you, Rupert," said Bobbin.

"At what?" asked Rupert.

"At a flying race."

Rupert laughed so long and so hard and so loud that the valley shook. He sneered at Bobbin and said, "You don't even have wings, and you think you can beat me in a flying race? I accept your challenge."

"Good!" answered Bobbin. "Come back here in two hours and we will be ready."

"Two hours it is!" said the dragon. Then he spread his huge wings and flew high into the sky and toward the mountains surrounding the valley.

"The Swangos began to give directions to the circus roustabouts and other circus hands. They only had two hours to get everything set up. The elephants helped to carry long poles that were used to hold up the circus tent. The platforms for the trapeze and high wire acts were set up in a big circle around the train. The swinging trapezes were hung from the wires and poles. There was a Swango on each of the trapeze bars, Bill, Doris, Robin and Dobbin. Bobbin Swango climbed onto a platform attached to a high pole with a waving flag on top.

"No sooner than Bobbin reached the platform, the sky grew dark with the shadow of Rupert the dragon as he flew toward the train.

"Your two hours are up. Are you ready for our race?" bellowed Rupert.

"Yes, I am. The race will be to fly one lap around the train."

"That's all?" laughed Rupert. "I'll win this race in no time at all. Then I will decide which of you to eat first!"

"The ringmaster climbed on top of the train. He cleared his throat and gave the race commands in his loud circus voice. "Is everybody ready? Take your marks . . . Get set. . . Go!"

"The dragon began to beat his mighty wings to slowly lift him off the ground. Bobbin Swango jumped off the platform and reached out her arms. As she began to fall, Robin Swango caught her hands as she swung from her swinging trapeze by the knees. They swung toward the next pole and Robin threw Bobbin through the air.

"The dragon was now high in the sky and he began to fly in a circle around the train. But Rupert was so big, that he had to take very wide turns, so he flew in a very wide circle.

"Meanwhile, Dobbin Swango next caught Bobbin and together they swung on the trapeze, and then Dobbin threw Bobbin through the air. Bobbin Swango curled up like a cannon ball and somersaulted through the air to

Doris Swango, who was swinging from a trapeze by her ankles. As the dragon flew high above, Doris swung with Bobbin and threw her through the air to Bill Swango.

"While Bill Swango swung through the air, Rupert was flying fast toward the finish and was gaining on Bobbin. Bill swung as high as he could and gave a mighty throw. As Bobbin curled up and spun through the air, she reached out her legs and landed on the platform where the race began. Bobbin had beat the dragon!

"Rupert landed by the platform and let out a tremendous bellow. Tears ran down his face and rolled off his long scaly snout. The tears sizzled as they crossed his fiery breath. "Nobody has ever defeated me before. The valley is now yours."

"The circus people laughed and cheered for Bobbin and the Swangos. They sang songs as they packed up the wires, poles, platforms, and trapeze swings that the Swangos had used to win the race. Rupert flew high into the mountains, and was never seen or heard from again."

"Is that the end of the story, GW?"

"Yes, it is."

"Then you're supposed to say, The End."

"The End. Goodnight Roberta."

"What's the mortal?"

"The mortal?"

"You know; the mortal of the story?"

"Oh, the *moral* of the story."

"That's what I said, GW. So what is it?"

"The moral of the story is that brains are better than brawn," GW explained.

"Oh. I thought it was that we should always fight monsters!" Roberta exclaimed.

"You know what Roberta? You just may be right."

"Goodnight, GW. Goodnight, Mommy."

"Goodnight, Bobbigirl," Ann Marie said. Then she kissed Roberta's forehead and we stepped outside of the room to give Roberta time to fall asleep.

In the cool night air, I dug my hands into my pockets and shifted from foot to foot. Ann Marie leaned against the door and looked as comfortable as if she were lying on a lounge chair.

"Ann Marie, I would like to ask you a question ordinarily taboo. How old are you?"

"I will be twenty-seven years old in exactly ten days. Why do you ask?"

"I'm curious how a young woman like you has amassed such an interesting history in such a relatively short period of time."

"I get it. What you really mean is: How did a nice girl like me get into a fix like this. Is that right?"

"Something like that," I admitted.

"GW, I'm an orphan by choice. Bobbie thinks her grandparents are all dead. As far as I know, they're all alive."

"How did you have such a falling out?"

"I was brought up in Wellesley, outside of Boston. Like everybody else in our neighborhood, we had a lot of money. My dad, Roger Sears, was a doctor. He stopped practicing medicine even before I was born and was involved in the stock market and real estate. He has the Midas touch when it comes to money. Every deal he ever touched turned to gold. And every person he ever touched was smeared with shit.

"My mother, Martha Smythe Conlon Sears, is an empty shell that I never knew. She was a beautiful woman with absolutely nothing inside. She kept herself trim and pretty, and drank vodka by the case. I don't believe either of my parents wanted children, but felt that they should have at least one for the sake of appearance. I don't remember ever hugging or kissing either of them.

"I was sent to boarding school at age thirteen. When I was fifteen, I left the Hutchison School For Girls the second day of the semester. I hitchhiked to Maine and worked as a waitress and maid at a Holiday Inn in

Portland. I got to share a room with another girl and was paid $50.00 a week. In the three months I worked there, I think I slept with almost every male guest who stayed at the place, not to mention the day manager, the night manager, and the bartender who used to give me booze to take to my room.

"I hitchhiked home for Thanksgiving. It was the first time my parents had heard from me since Labor Day. They asked me how school was going and when I had to be back. They had no idea that I hadn't been at school that entire semester. That evening I left the house and have not been back since."

"God, if one of my children disappeared, I would have been frantic. How can you be so callous? Your parents must have looked for you."

Ann Marie let out a good laugh.

"GW, until this week, I have never been more than about twenty miles away from my parents' house. At first, I stayed with a friend. I used to watch the news and read the paper for word that I was missing. They never looked for me. Once in a while I'll see my father's name in the Boston Globe in connection with some big project he's invested in or for some civic award he's received. I was never reported as missing. When I was a little girl I used to get an allowance. Every time my father handed me the five dollar bill he used to say, "Don't look a gift horse in the mouth." I guess my parents considered my disappearance a gift horse."

I did not know what to say to Ann Marie after that, so I didn't say anything. We stood outside for another five or ten minutes and then checked on Roberta. She was asleep, so Ann Marie and I turned in as well.

4. Meeting Old Friends

*A*t Roberta's request we returned to the Trainwreck Diner for breakfast the next morning. We decided to follow the coast through the Carolinas and into Georgia. I would start the day behind the wheel and Ann Marie would navigate. She wanted to make sure I did my share of the driving before it got dark. She had not forgotten the incident on Route One in Rhode Island. As I preferred to drive during the bright sun of the morning, I readily agreed.

We started south on Route 301 and then picked up Route 17, which we followed along the Rappahannock River. Rivers conjure romantic images in the historical and literary development of the country. Hudson, Potomac, Ohio, Mississippi, Colorado, Rio Grande: they all suggest events from bygone days. Now most rivers are merely wet brown strips to cross in an automobile at sixty-five miles an hour. They have lost their importance in commerce and travel. I feel a kinship to these rivers. I was once very important, at least to my family. Now they are gone. For a long time I was moderately important to the hundreds of students who hoped to do well in my class. Now I am a barely noticed old man who is merely an obstacle to be passed by those younger and stronger than myself.

We picked up Route 258 and crossed the James River. Roberta was tickled pink by the names of the towns of Tappahannock and Chuckatuck. We drove through a marshy area into North Carolina on Route 32. Ann Marie was a bit worried to be in a place called the Dismal Swamp Wildlife Refuge, but onward we rode over Albemarle Sound.

I drove west on Route 64 until we picked up Route 17, which we would take us all the way through South Carolina and into Savannah, Georgia. We passed Pollocksville, and stopped for lunch and a stretch in the town of Gregoryville. We walked past a drug store called Phillip's Pharmacy and Soda Shop. I had not seen a drug store with a lunch counter since the early 1950s and I convinced Ann Marie that we should eat there. As we sat on the round pedestal stools and watched our hamburgers fry on the grill, the only thing between us and our lunch was a white cracked Formica counter with green veins crisscrossing the surface. Ann Marie and I sipped strong coffee while Roberta spun in circles on her squeaky seat.

After our lunch we took a walk. We did not need our winter coats in the South Carolina sunshine. There was no trace of snow to be seen and both grass and trees held more than the occasional glimpse of green to be seen in the New England we had left behind. We passed a construction site where a small wood frame commercial building was going up. A sign in front said: "TEMP. HELP WANTED. NON-UNION JOB." Ann Marie put Roberta's hand in mine and told me to "Watch Bobbi for a minute." She walked over to a man that I supposed was the foreman. He was a tall man with a prodigious belly that hung over the wide leather belt holding up his blue jeans.

While he watched Ann Marie approach him he slid his baseball cap that said "BEECHNUT" back onto his head with one hand and rubbed his belly with the other.

"What kind of help are you looking for?" Ann Marie asked when she reached him. He spit a long stream of brown juice before answering.

"We're looking for rough carpenters. Know anybody who needs work?"

"You're looking at her. I do framing, rough and finish carpentry, painting, plastering and masonry. How long is the job?"

"Job ends when I get an occupancy permit for this building."

"That should be about ten work days, right?" Ann Marie said.

"That's right."

"What does the job pay?"

"Pay's eight dollars fifty an hour."

"I'm just passing through with my daughter and father. That's them over there," she said pointing to Roberta and myself. "You pay me six-fifty off the books and find a place to put us up and you got a deal. My tools are in my truck down the street."

"What's your name, Miss?"

"Ann Marie Fobbs."

"Please to meet you, Ms. Fobbs. My name is Tim Gristle. Folks call me T-Bone." He paused to spit another stream of tobacco juice before continuing. "I'll tell you what: I'll pay you eight-fifty an hour for the rest of the day. If you work out, we'll take it day by day. That sound okay to you?"

"I'll get my belt and be back in ten minutes. And thanks, T-Bone."

Ann Marie ran to me and told me I was sitter of the day. She got her tools and I got Roberta. Even when my children were young, I was not alone with my daughter Jenny for more than an hour or two at a time. And that was rare. It was not because I found my daughter disagreeable in any way. Quite the contrary, I doted on her. However, I am nothing if not a product of my times. I worked during the week and weekends when necessary. Kat stayed home with the children. When they were school age I would have a catch with my son and bring him and a few of his friends to the occasional ball game. Whatever parental guidance and wisdom my daughter needed, she received from Kat. As a result, I was not sure that I was particularly suited to the task at hand.

"So, Roberta, what would you like to do?" I asked. I hoped that the decision making would be handled by Roberta. I am not particularly proud of that, but in any event, it didn't work.

"I don't know, GW I'm not from around here."

"All right, Roberta, we shall go to one of my favorite places."

Ann Marie left the keys in the truck for us. I drove about the center of town until I found what I was looking for. I parked the truck and brought Roberta into the Caldwell Foster Memorial Library.

"Roberta," I explained, "I am a teacher. I have been a teacher most of my life. I would take great pleasure if you would allow me to teach you today."

"Okay, GW! I like school."

"What grade are you in?"

"I was in second grade, but I haven't gone to school for a while."

"You are in luck, Roberta. I have an excellent second grade curriculum." I assured her.

"GW, I don't even know what a cricklem is! You told me you would use easy words."

"You're right. But now that I am your teacher, I will teach you a new word. The word is Cur-rick-u-lum. Can you say that?"

"Cur-rick-u-lum."

"Excellent. Curriculum means a series of required

studies. Now, let's go inside."

One thing I love about this country is that almost every single town has its own library. In a small town it is often the prettiest public building. Most of the users are school age children and retired men and women. What a shame that fewer and fewer people feel the need to go into a library. The church-like atmosphere of whispers and turning pages gives me a feeling of calm as soon as I walk through the door.

Roberta and I walked into the Children's section and sat at a low table.

"Roberta, what kind of books do you read in school?"

"We use a second grade reader and work book, but I don't really like it very much."

"Why is that?"

"Those books are too boring. And the teacher goes so slow I can't even stand it! Mrs. Grapple got mad at me because I finished my whole workbook."

"Why would your teacher be angry with you for finishing your workbook? Did you scribble in it?"

"No. I just filled in all the answers, but she said it was supposed to last the whole year, not just one week."

"You did the whole year's reading in one week?"

"No, GW, don't be silly. That's just when Mrs. Grapple saw that my book was filled in! I did it the second day of class."

"Roberta, we may be wasting our time in the children's section. Why don't we pick a book from the young adult section and see how you do?"

"Okay, GW. That sounds like fun!"

I perused the shelves until I found a book by S.E. Hinton called *The Outsiders*. We went into a corner of the children's section and I asked Roberta to begin reading the book aloud to me. It was shocking to hear how beautifully she read. Every once in a while she would ask me the meaning of a word, or I would ask her what she thought about a particular passage. Roberta enjoyed the names

Ponyboy, Darry, and Two Bit. She rolled them around in her mouth the first time she read them. Several hours had passed when I looked out a window and noticed it was dark.

Roberta and I gathered our coats and left. Roberta told me that *The Outsiders* was the "best book she ever read in her entire life." For me, it felt good to teach again. We drove to the construction site where Ann Marie sat waiting for us on a stack of plywood.

"Hi, Bobbigirl. Did you and GW have fun today?"

"We sure did! GW let me read a whole book to him, and it was way better than the baby stories I used to get at school."

"Good. Give your mommy a big hug and congratulate me. I got the job."

"Congratulations, Ann Marie. Does your job include a room or should we find a local motel?" I asked.

"No need. We can share a room at T-Bone's mother's house. T-Bone said she'll feed us too. I could use a home cooked meal."

"Excellent. Where does Mrs. Bone live?" I asked.

"Don't be a wise guy, GW. Her name is Mrs. Edna Gristle, and I have directions to her house. It's only a few miles. I'll drive."

Ann Marie drove and I read the directions that T-Bone had written out. We moved from a two-lane blacktop, to a narrower gravel road, and then onto a dirt road for the final half mile. Roberta enjoyed the bumpy ride on the rutted dirt road and asked if we could drive over it again.

"Not tonight, Bobbigirl. And you be on your best behavior, got it?" Ann Marie warned her daughter.

"You bet!"

"And remember, Honey, GW is my father, and your grandfather, okay?"

"Can I still call him GW?" Roberta wanted to know.

"Of course you can." I answered for Ann Marie.

We stopped in front of a large clapboard house that

looked like it had been built in sections. The main house was a modest two story home. Attached to it were sections of house, some with two floors, and some with only one. They shot out from the sides and back and veered off at odd angles. The three of us climbed the worn steps of the front porch and the door opened before we even had a chance to ring the bell. We were greeted by perhaps the largest woman I had ever seen.

Mrs. Gristle stood about six feet, three inches, so we looked each other more or less in the eye. But whereas I was merely a stretched out welterweight, Edna Gristle was a bona fide heavyweight. She weighed no less than three hundred and fifty pounds. Her hair was dyed a bright orange that probably approximated the color of her hair when she was a young girl. When she shook my hand, I feared that she would crush it.

Edna Gristle was big all over and as strong as a bear. Yet she did not look the least bit masculine. She had formidable breasts and wide hips and wore a dress covered by an apron with a large pocket in front. The apron was embroidered with flowers and the legend, "NOBODY LEAVES MY HOUSE HUNGRY." The large embroidered letters were able to fit on one line across her bosom with room to spare.

"C'mon and get inside, you folks must be hungry. My baby told me you been drivin' for days," Edna said as she herded us into her kitchen. She was shaking my hand, hugging Ann Marie and Roberta, and tending several pots and pans all at the same time.

"And who might your baby be, Mrs. Gristle?" I asked.

"My baby is T-Bone. I know he's a grown man but he's the runt of the litter. He's so tiny I can't help but to think of him as a baby. And don't you Mrs. Gristle me. My name is Edna."

"It's a pleasure to meet you, Edna. Please call me George."

"We really appreciate you putting us up, Edna" Ann

Marie said.

"Oh, it's my sincere pleasure, Annie. I hardly ever get to cook for more than myself any more, except weekends of course. Now you folks wash up down the hall and come on back into the kitchen for supper. I'll get y'all settled in after that. Now go!"

Not even Ann Marie would dare disobey an order from Edna, so we did as we were told and then returned to the kitchen. Edna had set warm, homemade biscuits on the table along with a stick of butter, a pitcher of water and a gallon of milk.

"You start on them biscuits now before they cool. I'll join you as soon as I get everything on the table." As I spread the butter on the biscuit I realized that it was probably the first time in years I had used butter rather than some bland corn oil margarine. Between bites of her biscuit Roberta managed to say to Ann Marie, "Mommy, did you know that bread could come warm?"

Edna laughed out loud at that and Ann Marie's face turned crimson.

"Mind your manners, *Roberta.*"

Edna put plates of fried chicken, baked potatoes, okra and green beans on the table.

"Don't be shy now, start eating," she ordered. And to ensure that she was obeyed, Edna put a large helping of everything on our plates. She then piled her plate with food and began eating with gusto. Edna Gristle is a woman who truly enjoys eating. Between swallows she asked some questions.

"Annie, T-Bone tells me that you're pretty good swingin' a hammer. That's a big compliment from him. How'd a little slip of a thing like you get into the trades?"

"My ex-husband was a carpenter. He taught me how and I used to work with him."

"That's good. I like a woman that can do a man's work. I can do the work of five good men even on a bad day. How about you, George? What do you do?"

"I'm retired, Edna. I used to teach English at The College of the Holy Cross in Worcester, Massachusetts."

"You're a teacher and your daughter is a carpenter? That's a good one!" Edna chuckled. "Where's your wife, George?"

"She passed away not too long ago."

"Sorry to hear that. My Henry died too. He got himself shot in a fight over at Swifty's. But Lord, those three boys he beat up will never be the same."

"He got shot while beating up three men?"

"Well, Henry was sixty-six years old. A couple years earlier and they never would have even been able to shoot him. When Henry hit you, you stayed hit." Edna chuckled a little and turned her attention to Roberta.

"So, little girl, how are you enjoying the ride from up North?"

"I'm having a lot of fun. It gets a little boring in the truck sometimes, though."

"What was the best thing you saw so far?"

"Oh, that was when my mommy beat up those two guys that tried to steal our stuff from the truck."

When Roberta said that I froze and Ann Marie started coughing.

"Bobbigirl, don't you start making up stories," Ann Marie said after a swallow of water.

"I'm not making up stories, Mommy. Don't you remember?"

Ann Marie cut her off and said, "Kids... They have such vivid imaginations."

Edna Gristle was not fooled for a second. "Looks like there's more to you than meets the eye, Annie. If you beat up some punks trying to rob you, then I guess they had it coming. I believe in live and let live. And I can see that little Bobbi is your girl. But I don't believe for a minute that the professor is your daddy. T-Bone believed you, but that boy is overly trusting. I'm glad to let you stay here, but not if you're on the run from the law. Now, are you on the run or not?"

Ann Marie was clearly nonplussed, so I decided to answer Edna truthfully. I would not have dared lie and risk incurring her wrath.

"Edna, I do not believe that the law is after us."

"Now what kind of an answer is that, George. It is or it ain't. There ain't no halfway here."

"Edna, this is what happened." I then told her about how Ann Marie and I met in court, the subsequent run-ins with Christian Lovett, and the hoodlums in Maryland. Edna never once interrupted me except to ask me to pass the ketchup. When I was finished with our story, Edna daintily wiped her lips with her napkin and said, "Welcome to my home. You can stay as long as you need to. I won't tell anybody what you told me. But let me tell you folks, Southern don't mean stupid. You'll make your life a lot less complicated around here if you tell the truth from here on. And that's about all the free advice you'll get from me. Now Bobbi, how about you help me clean up?"

"Okay, Mrs. Gristle."

After cleaning up, we brought our valises in from the truck, except for Ann Marie's tools, which she would need early the next morning. Edna offered us each our own room, but Ann Marie and Roberta chose to stay together in one room. I had the room across the hall. I stayed in the parlor with Edna chatting while Ann Marie went upstairs to put Roberta to bed.

"How many children do you have, Edna?"

"I gave birth to six live children, all boys. Henry Junior died in infancy and the other five are all living nearby. How about you, George?"

"I had two, a son and daughter. Both are gone."

"Sorry to hear that, George. Gone to the bosom of Jesus, though..."

"All in all, I would rather have them here on earth."

"Amen to that, George. So what do you plan on doing in Florida?"

"I'm not certain. I suppose that I'll be able to get my social security benefits started up again. Maybe I'll find part time work teaching. I had forgotten how much I loved it until I spent today at the library with Roberta. I believe she's a very gifted child. And what do you do with yourself, Edna?"

"I stay here in this house. Hank was born here, and so was his dad. After I go, I hope one of my kids will stay on. There's about sixty-five acres with this place. None of my kids are farmers, so I rent the fields cheap to the people next door. At least the land is being worked. I couldn't live with myself if it got all overgrown. My kids and grandkids come over on weekends and the house fills up with my family. That's my favorite time. You'll probably meet a bunch of them this weekend."

We were interrupted by Ann Marie. She informed me that Roberta was tucked in and had requested another story from me. I was thrilled. I excused myself and ascended the stairs to find Roberta.

"What kind of story would you like to hear tonight, Roberta?" I asked.

"Something about you, GW," she said.

"I'm not a very interesting subject. Maybe there's something else you would like to hear." Roberta would have none of that.

"No, no, no, GW. I want to hear a story about you. You're one of my favorite people, you know."

"I suppose I would need a heart of stone to refuse a request like that. All right, I'll tell you a story about me.

"Once upon a time, long ago, there was a young man named George Wellington Hodge. As you know, Roberta, that man was me. The year was 1945, and the month was October. I had been a soldier in a big war that had just ended, and had just arrived home. It felt wonderful to be in civvies again."

"What are civvies, GW?"

"Civvies are civilian clothes...anything other than an

army uniform. My family treated me like a celebrity. On my first day back my mother had a big party for me. Friends, relatives, and neighbors jammed into our small house. Some of the people I had last seen as little boys and girls were now grown up men and women, and I did not immediately recognize them. I looked different as well. They had last seen me as a fresh-faced eighteen-year-old boy. Now they saw that I was a twenty-two-year-old man. But that was only on the outside. On the inside, I felt very old. It was as if I had aged ten years on the inside for each year I was away from home.

"I was somewhat overwhelmed by all of the attention I was receiving. My own home, the house I grew up in, seemed very strange to me. It was as if I was a visitor from another country who understood the language spoken, but not the meaning. I was beginning to feel very sad, when I saw the most beautiful girl that I had ever seen. Her name was Katherine Franklin, and she was the cousin of our next door neighbor. She just happened to be visiting that day, so she was brought to the party.

"Katherine did not know many people at the party, and I noticed her sitting alone outside under a maple tree eating a piece of cake. The leaves on the tree were past the peak of color and were turning a golden brown. Some had already fallen, forming a speckled circle around the tree trunk, but most of the leaves were still on the tree. Katherine was wearing a white blouse with a green button down sweater over it. She had a woolen green plaid skirt that went halfway between her knees and ankles.

"Roberta, when I saw Katherine, I thought my heart would stop. It was love at first sight!"

"Did Katherine love you at first sight too?"

"I don't think so. Katherine did not see me that day. You see, I was afraid to talk to her. Instead, I asked the people I knew at the party, "Who is the redhead with the white blouse and green sweater?" Finally, my neighbor, Jimmy Pender, told me she was his little cousin. I found out from him where she lived and where she worked. She was a teller at the Worcester County Institute For Savings in downtown Worcester. The next day I opened a savings account there. I found a reason to be there every day, and I always stood in Katherine's line. Finally, one day I got the nerve to ask her out on a date. And do you know what she said to me?"

"No, GW. What?" Roberta asked.

"She said, "I was wondering when you would finally get up the nerve to ask me out, George. Sure I'll go out with you." And five months later, Katherine Franklin and I were married. And that, Roberta, is the story about how I met my wife. Now go to sleep and I'll see you in the morning."

I covered Roberta with the blanket and shut off the light. As I was about to walk out of the room Roberta scolded me. "GW, where do you think you are going?"

"I'm going downstairs now, Roberta."

"But you forgot to kiss me goodnight!" she pointed out.

I promised to make it up to her by giving her two kisses, one on each cheek. Then I kissed her goodnight and left the room. It was reassuring to have a family again.

5. Hammer Swinger

I was awakened at dawn the next morning by a rooster. At first I was disoriented by the crowing and by the blue paint on the walls and shelf full of sports trophies above the small wood desk. For a wonderful moment, I thought I was in my son's room as it was in his youth. The moment passed and I went down the stairs to the kitchen, which was already a hive of activity. Ann Marie was seated in front of the tallest stack of pancakes I had ever seen. The table was burdened by a pitcher of orange juice, among plates of pancakes, sausages and eggs. A pot of coffee percolated on the counter making the hollow bubbling noise that has been largely replaced by the hiss of drip coffee makers. Edna got up from the table as I walked into the kitchen and poured me a cup of coffee.

"I thought you were going to sleep the day away, George! Get up and at 'em. Sit down and eat so we can figure out what you're going to do today."

"Edna, this coffee is wonderful. I will pass on the eggs

and sausages, if you don't mind. My doctor has advised me that I should cut back on fat and cholesterol," I informed her.

"George, for a former teacher you have no sense at all. You're about a day older than dirt, you don't have a pot to piss in or a window to throw it out, and you have no idea where you're going to be in a day, never mind a month or a year. Your family is all gone, and you're worried about high cholesterol? Do you like sausages and eggs?" she demanded.

"Yes, I do" I admitted.

"Then snap out of it and eat, George! For crying out loud, you don't have the sense the Good Lord gave a newt."

There was only one thing I could say. "Ann Marie, please pass the eggs."

Ann Marie laughed and slid them over to me.

"Edna called T-Bone and told him to pick me up this morning, so you can have the truck. Maybe you can take Bobbi to the library again. She liked that."

"I would be glad to, unless there is anything around here that Edna would like me to do to help out."

"You must be joking," Edna said. "Any time a man tries to help out I just have twice as much work to do. Take Bobbi to the library in the morning and then come back here in the afternoon so we can talk. It seems like I hardly ever get to talk to a man close to my age anymore."

Roberta walked into the kitchen rubbing her eyes. Ann Marie poured her some juice, filled up a plate and told her that she would be going to the library with me.

"Okay, Mommy. I like the library. Can we read another book today, GW?" she asked me.

"I am quite sure that we can. We'll drive there after you help Mrs. Gristle clean up breakfast."

We listened to the sound of a truck driving down the dirt road toward the house. A horn blew and Edna informed us that T-Bone had arrived to pick up Ann

Marie. She picked up her jacket and tool belt, kissed Roberta goodbye and was out the door.

"Edna", I asked, "how did your son get the nickname T-Bone?"

"Oh that", she laughed. "Tim hated his name since he was a little boy. He's the youngest and the smallest to boot. One Christmas when he was about five, one of his brothers took to callin' him Tiny Tim, after that crippled boy in *A Christmas Carol*. That was just too much for him to bear.

"I asked the boys to leave him alone, but you know how boys are. Well, one night we were sitting down to dinner and my boy Red turns to Tim and says, 'Hey, Tiny Tim, pass the ketchup.' Well, we were eating steak and Tim grabbed the T-Bone off his plate and hit Red in the forehead with it and knocked him off his chair. Since then we've called him T-Bone. Tim likes that name just fine."

"You have a colorful family, Edna. You mentioned T-Bone and Red. Are any of your sons called by their given name?"

"Just Horace. The other four go by T-Bone, Red, Pie and LB."

"I hope I get to meet them, Edna. How is it that Horace doesn't have a nickname?"

"If you meet him, you'll find out," Edna said. And then she laughed and shook her head to a private joke.

While I was at the library with Roberta, Ann Marie was working on the third floor of the incipient office building. T-Bone introduced her to the crew chief working on drywall and stairwells. Ann Marie stood before a six foot three inch whip of a man who looked to be anywhere between fifty and seventy. His iron gray crewcut erupted from his scalp and looked as if it could double as a weapon. He extended a gnarled hand to Ann Marie and said, "I'm JR Stone, and you'll be working with me today." They walked toward a group of three younger men drinking coffee from thermos cups at the south end of the site.

"The fattish boy with the beard is Bobby. He's good people. The longhaired boy is AJ and he's mine, so you let me know if he ain't polite. The dude with the slick hair and moustache is Denny. He don't have much sense, but he's reliable and does what he's told."

JR made introductions all around.

"I'm looking forward to working with you guys," Ann Marie said.

"Same here," replied Denny.

"Alright, now let's get to it. Denny and AJ you're with me in the south stairs. Bobby, you start on the second floor with Annie."

"Okay, boss. C'mon with me, Annie; it's going to be a busy day."

Back in the young adult section of the library, I left Roberta reading *Charlie and the Chocolate Factory*. I went to the front desk and asked the librarian, Miss Renner, if they had any elementary and junior high school mathematics textbooks. She retrieved some for me and then I committed a modern day *faux pas*. I said, "Thank you, Miss Renner."

In as cold a voice as I have ever heard, I was informed "I am not a *Miss*".

"Excuse me. Thank you, Mrs. Renner," I said, foolishly assuming that I was mistaken as to her marital status.

"No sir, it is *Mizz*. The polite way to address me is *Mizz* Renner."

"Are you married?" I asked.

"As a matter of fact, I am not. But that is irrelevant."

"It is entirely relevant. It is both proper and polite to address an unmarried woman as Miss. As in, 'Thank you, Miss.' There is absolutely nothing rude or demeaning about such a form of address."

"Irregardless, sir, I prefer to be addressed as *Mizz*."

"When you phrase it so eloquently, how could I possibly refuse your request, Mizz Renner. Sorry for the *mizz*take." I shook my head in dismay at the rough handling to which the English language is subjected and returned to Roberta with the textbooks.

I perused the math texts and copied some problems from each. I admit, I only used problems to which the book supplied answers. After addition, subtraction, multiplication and division, I do not have much confidence in my own mathematical skills.

I gave the sheets of paper with the problems to Roberta and asked her to do as many as she could. The first problems were from a fourth grade book and the final problems were from a ninth grade text. I even included two-word problems. While Roberta worked at the problems, I read the copy of a New York Times kept in the circulation section. An hour later, Roberta handed me the papers. The addition, multiplication, subtraction and long division problems showed only the correct answer after the equal sign. There was no scratch work at all. It was the same with fractions and decimals. The word problems and algebra problems were all completed flawlessly.

"Roberta, this is very good. Did you ever encounter this type problem in school?"

"Sure, GW. We did addition and subtraction. But I like the other problems better; they're way more fun."

"How did you know how to do the fractions, multiplication and division?"

"I just picture the problem in my head and solve it."

"I believe we're done for the day, Roberta," I said. "Let's head back to Mrs. Gristle's house."

"Goody! She said she had cold chicken for lunch!"

After a delicious lunch of cold fried chicken, cranberry sauce, and homemade potato salad followed by homemade apple pie, Edna and I sat in the living room to talk.

Roberta stayed in the kitchen and puzzled over problems from a junior high school math text borrowed from the library.

"So tell me, George, what became of your family? Annie told me about your son. What happened to your daughter?"

I sat back for a few moments collecting my thoughts about Jenny. To her credit, Edna did not say a word. She just waited until I was ready to talk.

"My daughter's name was Jenny. By the time she was thirteen she insisted that I call her Jennifer, so I did. But I always think of her as Jenny.

"Jenny was a pretty girl from the day she was born. That was during the summer of 1950. Right from the first day of her life, Jenny had a knack for twisting me around her finger. I do not believe that I ever once raised my voice to my daughter. Of course, my wife was in charge of discipline and such. Nevertheless, to use a tired phrase, Jenny truly was the apple of my eye.

"Jenny did well throughout school. She grew to be the image of her mother, and that was beautiful indeed. She graduated from the University of Massachusetts at Amherst in June 1971 and immediately left to drive around the country with her boyfriend in an old station wagon. I was somewhat upset that she was going to be traveling with a man to whom she was not married. Jenny said that she would see the country in part as a tribute to her brother Michael, who had planned such a trip but never had the chance to complete it.

"Eventually, Jenny settled down to a career as a teacher for the fourth grade at the Martin E. Young School in Randolph, Massachusetts. In 1983, when she was thirty-three years old, she finally became engaged to be married. While she was engaged, she went to see her doctor about a lump she had felt on her breast. She was diagnosed with breast cancer. Moreover, it had already spread into her lymph nodes. Jenny was married two months later in a small ceremony at my home. Two months after that, she was gone."

Edna shook her head and sighed.

"Ain't nothing on this earth worse than losing a child. I'm so sorry for you, George, losing two like you did."

"Thank you, Edna. There's always an ache, like a shadow over my heart, for my children. Usually, I don't notice it, and then I'll see a little girl or boy who reminds me in some way of my children. Or even worse, I'll meet a man or woman who are the age that my children would be now. Then I try to picture what Jenny or Michael would look like, and I can't."

"What about Ann Marie or Bobbi? Do either of them remind you of your Jenny?"

"No. Both are such unique and interesting people, I don't believe I have ever met anybody else remotely like them. This morning at the library, Roberta showed a remarkable facility with math problems up to high school level. She has less than two years of formal education. I have had thousands of students, and not one was nearly as gifted as she."

"Do you think Ann Marie knows that?"

"She must realize that Roberta is very bright. Ann Marie is quite intelligent herself. I don't know if she realizes the extent of Roberta's gift. Neither do I, for that matter. I believe I've barely begun to scratch the surface of her capabilities."

"What are you going to do about it?"

"I'm not sure I follow you, Edna. What can I do about Roberta's intelligence?"

"That girl needs some guidance and teaching. You're a teacher. Are you going to tutor her?"

"I hadn't thought about it. My plans don't go beyond reaching Florida. After that, I'll figure something out. Also, I don't know if Ann Marie would want that. Roberta's schooling has to be Ann Marie's decision."

"I know that, George. But you could help Annie make

the decision. Suggest it to her. She respects your opinion, and she's fond of you."

"I'll have to think about that."

"I think it's a great idea for you to tutor me, GW," Roberta shouted from the kitchen door.

"Bobbi, how long have you been listening to me and George talk?" Edna demanded.

"Long enough to hear GW tell you how smart I am. I want GW to be my teacher. He's interesting. School was boring."

"Roberta," I explained, "if I tutor you, there will be no children your age to play with. There is only so much I can give you. I cannot play with you as your school mates would."

"GW, you're silly! Just because you teach me doesn't mean I can't play with kids my own age and do other stuff too. Don't you like teaching me in the library?"

"I enjoy it more than anything else I have done in many years, Roberta."

Roberta then ran to me and threw her arms around my neck and hugged me. I knew then that I would do everything in my power to convince Ann Marie to allow me to tutor her.

That evening at dinner Ann Marie told us about her run in at work with Denny Frick.

"I was hammering a section of plywood on the outer wall when Denny Frick's hand rubbed across my breasts after reaching across me to take some nails from a box. "Excuse me, Annie, I didn't mean to touch you there," he said.

"It's all right, Denny." I told him, and I just kept hammering like nothing had happened.

"Then Denny bent down to tie his shoes. When he finished, he reached back to the nail box. That time he definitely copped a feel—kind of left his hand there and squeezed a little. I just kept hammering. Well, he must've been encouraged by that because he gave up any pretense and stood behind me and reached in front of me and squeezed my boobs.

"So I turned around and put my hand over his crotch, and I leaned close to his ear and whispered, "Do you like this, Denny?" And he said, "Oh yeah, baby." So I said to him, "Do you want to give it to me?" Now, he was breathin' heavy and grunted at me, "You know I do, baby."

"So I unzipped his pants and pulled out his . . ." She glanced at Roberta before she continued. "I leaned in to whisper in his ear again, and now he had his eyes closed— he just can't believe his luck. He even mumbled something like, "All those Saturday nights wasted in bars buying drinks for women and getting nothing., and now here I am at work about to get my pole waxed..."

He could feel my breath in his ear as I whispered, "Look down, Denny." He looked down and his eyes bugged out because I was holding a pliers open around the base of his dick. "What the hell do you think you're doing?" he yelled as he tried to push me away. I just closed the pliers a bit, and Denny froze. I said, "Look, you really are in no position to be talking to me that way, do you understand me?" By this time he was pretty frantic and said to me, "Yes ma'am," real nice and polite. So I said, "Good. Now, do you think you're ever going to want to use that pathetic excuse for a pecker again?" And he said, "Oh yes, ma'am." So I said, "Then listen to me very closely. I do not want you to ever touch me again. Do you understand? In fact, I don't want you to even think about touching me again. Do you understand me, Denny?"

"Yes I understand," he said.

I loosened the grip with the pliers and he quickly zipped his pants and took off. I watched him run and started to laugh when I heard T-Bone's voice from the fourth floor.

"Miss Annie Fobbs, I do believe I can stop worrying about you now," he said. I asked him how long he'd been there and he told me, "Long enough. I figured it was only a matter of time until Denny tried something. That boy is singularly unlucky at love."

So I thanked him for letting me handle it myself, and he said, "Go wash them damn pliers, will you?"

Ann and Edna laughed until tears streamed down their faces.

"That boy has the worst luck with women of anybody I have ever known. How did you ever think to grab his thing with a pliers, Annie?"

"Edna, I don't plan much of anything. One minute he was coming onto me, and the next I had his pecker in my pliers."

They both started laughing again and the table shook as Edna slapped the top while she guffawed. Roberta continued to eat without paying much attention to her mother or Edna. Roberta looked at me and said, "Are you going to ask her, GW?"

"Ask who what?" I wanted to know.

"Ask my mom about tutoring me?"

Ann Marie put down her fork and looked at me.

"What's this about, GW?"

"Ann Marie," I began, "you must have noticed that Roberta is a very bright girl."

"Sure, she gets all A's in school, and I know she can read just about anything."

"Yes, but it goes beyond that. Over the past few days at the library, I have discovered that Roberta reads at least at a junior high school level, and she can do math problems beyond the Junior High School level. That includes algebra problems, fractions, and other problems that Roberta has never seen in school."

"Really? That's great. How come you never told me that, Bobbigirl?"

"I never did that kind of stuff before, Mommy. GW found the books for me to use in the library."

Ann Marie shook her head and then looked at me. "So,

what do you have in mind, GW?"

"If it is acceptable to you, I would like to tutor Roberta."

"That's okay while we're here and on the road, but what about when we get to Florida? We never discussed where in Florida we're going, or how we're going to live, or anything else. I figured that Bobbie would go to school wherever we live. She has to go to school not only to get an education, but to meet other kids and get involved in sports and all the other things that kids do."

"I do not have any definite plans for what I will do when I get to Florida. If you don't mind having me around, I can help out with Roberta's schooling and take care of her while you are at work. What I suggest is that we try it for now and see how things work out. At some point, Roberta should probably enter into a program for gifted children."

"What do you mean, GW?"

"I mean that your daughter is probably a genius."

6. The Gristles

Ann Marie worked for T-Bone for the next few weeks, and on Friday, March 4, 1994 the town of Gregoryville issued the occupancy permit for the building.

"I guess the job is up, T-Bone; thanks for giving me a chance."

"This job is over, Annie, but I have other work lined up. You have a job here as long as I can get work. You were about the best man I had on the job."

"Thank you, but I do mean to get to Florida. Besides, GW's counting on me for the ride and Bobbi has grown very attached to him."

"Well, if you change your mind, I'd love to have you back. Take the weekend to think about it, because you can't leave until Monday anyway. Ma's planning on you folks being here this Sunday to meet everybody. Every Gristle in the county will be there."

"I wouldn't miss that for the world. I can't wait to meet your brother Horace."

T-Bone laughed and said, "Don't count on that, Annie. I'll see you Sunday."

Sunday was a cool dry day. Bits of winter clung to the ground, but spring was making its presence felt too. Edna served an early breakfast of cereal, muffins, eggs, juice and coffee. That constituted a starvation diet in the Gristle household. As soon as the breakfast dishes were cleared away, Edna began to cook for her clan. I still find it difficult to believe that a woman of her size could move so quickly and gracefully. Butter was drawn on the stove while ovens heated and turkeys were cleaned and hams dressed. She chopped, peeled, washed, diced and sliced vegetables and fruits and refused all offers of assistance. Pies baked, and then cooled while potatoes, yams and muffins filled the two ovens and fireplace. Pots and pans were cleaned and put away as soon as empty so the large kitchen was never messy or cluttered. All the while Edna kept up her end of a lively conversation with Ann Marie, Roberta and me.

Shortly after eleven, the Gristles began to arrive. Most came in pick-up trucks with two or three adults in the cab and several children riding in the bed. A few sedans and jeeps arrived too, as well as one motorcycle with sidecar. The trucks were parked haphazardly in the yard and became playground toys for the Gristle children. Roberta watched in wonder as more children than she had ever seen in one place played ball, wrestled, ran around and made noise. After failing to convince Roberta to join in with the other children, Edna called in one of her grandchildren, Susie Sue, who looked to be about ten years old.

"Susie Sue, this is Roberta Fobbs. I'm assigning her to you. It's your job to make sure that she has fun and that nobody else kills her. Now go on!"

"Yes, Grandma," mumbled Susie Sue. She then grabbed Roberta by the hand and ran outside dragging Roberta behind her.

I was watching Roberta play with the other children when I heard the rumble of a deuce and a half-truck bouncing down the dirt road. It was obviously a military truck and still painted in a camouflage design. I had not seen a truck like it since 1945. The driver of the truck leaned on the horn, which played *Dixie*. The truck skidded to a halt in a cloud of dust. Out of the cloud emerged the largest man I had ever seen. He was seven and a half feet tall and easily five hundred pounds. His face was hidden by a thick brown beard that started just under his eyes, skirted his nose, and disappeared into a flannel shirt. I looked behind him half expecting to see a huge blue ox, but he was followed only by his petite red-haired wife and several children.

"Mama, I'm hungrier than a bear; when do we eat?" the behemoth demanded. The children laughed and ran around him, between his legs and into him as he walked toward the house. Occasionally a child would ricochet off him and tumble several feet. He stopped at a blue pick-up truck and shouted, "T-Bone, you runt, I told you not to park this piece of tin on the walk!" He lifted the front end of the truck three feet high and pushed it like a wheelbarrow out of his way. When he reached his mother on the porch he put his hands on her hips and picked her up to kiss her on the forehead. He placed Edna back on the ground as if he were handling a child.

"George, I'd like to introduce you to my boy Horace. Horace, this is George Hodge."

"I'm pleased to meet you, Horace."

"So you're the professor that's been enjoying my mama's hospitality?" he asked.

"Yes, I am," I answered as a crowd gathered around the porch.

"Then I want to know what your intentions are, and they damn well better be honorable!"

"Indeed they are. I've been staying with your mother while the woman I'm traveling with worked for your brother. We're leaving tomorrow."

"So you just use my mama and take off with another woman! Who do you think you're dealing with, professor? Do right by mama and marry her. T-Bone, Red, Pie, LB and me will see to it, ain't that right, Mama?"

"Horace, leave the poor man alone. He doesn't know you well enough to tell when you're kiddin'" Edna told him.

"I'm just being friendly, Mama. Where's that Annie girl that T-Bone told me about?"

"I'm right here, Horace," said Annie as she walked out of the kitchen.

"A little thing like you swings a hammer for a living? I don't believe it. One of my legs weighs more than you."

"I'm stronger than I look, Horace. You better be polite or I may have to teach you some manners."

"Hell, she's feisty, T-Bone. No wonder Denny Frick went home with his tail between his legs."

"He almost went home without it at all," said Ann Marie.

For the next two or three hours I enjoyed the semi-controlled bedlam of the Gristle Family. Infants clung to mothers who chatted while setting up picnic tables outside. The younger children played games of tag, Red Rover, King of the Hill, and ran, climbed, jumped and scrambled on, over and through everything and everyone. Several teenagers raced mini-bikes, three wheelers and a tractor in a fenced-in acre of mud. All of the men except Horace and me retreated to the barn to talk and drink. Horace mingled with the different groups of youngsters. With the toddlers, he was a large, hairy jungle gym. Young Gristles climbed up his legs and over his back and shoulders. I even saw a young girl hanging by his beard. The children swung, climbed and kicked with abandon. When a boy or girl would occasionally fall from Horace, he softly caught them in one callused hand.

Horace moved to a group of older children who looked

to be about ten to twelve. He wrestled with them and tossed them high in the air and caught them as they fell. The boys and girls laughed and took turns taking rides. Finally, Horace moved into a group of a dozen teenage boys and a few girls.

Horace bellowed, "You miserable, lazy, weak bunch of loafers! The sight of you candy asses makes me sick!"

On cue, the entire group of Gristle adolescents leaped at Horace. The giant could not be seen under the pile as a squirming mound of bodies spun and lurched. A boy flew off the pile and landed heavily six feet away. He ran back to the mound and dove on, and immediately disappeared into the vibrating mass.

The bodies on top of Horace slid down until only his legs were covered. He fell like a tree, and I swear I felt the ground shake thirty yards away. After several minutes a scream emanated from the pile that was not quite human. Bodies flew out of the ball of arms and legs as if from a catapult. Horace stood at the center of prone teenagers, slightly bloody and grinning. He shook his head sadly and looked at his attackers.

"Damn! They just don't make Gristles as tough as they used to." He then brushed off his clothes and walked away. His nieces, nephews, sons and daughters rose somewhat more gingerly.

At three o'clock, Edna rang the triangle dinner bell and the Gristle clan began to find seats at the picnic tables. The adults sat at two tables, the older teenagers with family infants at two more, and another for the younger children. Edna, Ann and the wives of the Gristle boys brought out the food. The tables creaked as heavy platters of turkey, ham, corn, okra, gravy, and biscuits were laid down. Pitchers of milk and lemonade were set out as well as bottles of beer. Nobody moved until everything was set out and Horace led the gathering in grace.

"Dear Father, thank you for the bounty you have given the Gristles. We're happy to share with the Professor,

Annie, Roberta and any other kind strangers you send our way. Amen."

The yard was filled with laughter and simultaneous conversations. Platters of food were laid out and they disappeared just as quickly. Eventually hams, roasts and turkeys were replaced by pies, cakes and coffee. The food subdued the Gristles physically, but the conversation remained animated.

After ten o'clock, the Gristles began to disperse. They bid us goodbye, and T-Bone repeated his offer of a job to Ann. The following morning Edna fixed us another big breakfast and gave us leftovers for lunch.

"Thank you, Edna; I've enjoyed our evening talks. If you don't mind, I would like to write to you when we get settled."

"That'd be fine, George. I'll warn you, I'm not a great letter writer myself, but I do enjoy reading mail that ain't bills. Your letters will be appreciated."

Edna hugged Ann and Roberta and walked us to the truck. Roberta was excited to be on the move again, and Ann let me drive because her eyes were a bit moist. After we cleared Gregoryville, Ann turned to me and said, "This was the first time I ever saw a family I would want to be a part of. I always thought that family talk was bullshit. You know, GW, I'm kind of sad for myself that I missed that. I hope I can give some of that to Bobbi."

"I have no doubt that you will, Ann. For most of my life, my family was the most important thing on earth to me. It was the cause of my greatest joys and most bitter moments of despair. I know that my life with them, even for a while, is better than it would have been without them."

"At least you had all those years of enjoying your family, GW. I know the hurt of your losses must be awful, but most of the years were good, weren't they?"

"They were, Ann. Something I am sad about is that the Hodge name dies with me. I have no brothers or sisters, and my children both died childless. It makes me feel my mortality even more keenly."

"That's why I keep a close eye on Bobbi. She means the world to me."

"She always will."

We drove in silence and almost missed the sign on the highway that told us we had reached our destination: "Welcome to Florida."

7. Home Schooled

"*S*top at that rest area!" Roberta yelled. I swerved into the area across a lane of traffic.

"What's wrong, Bobbigirl?" Ann asked.

"Just let me out!" Roberta yelled as she catapulted out of the truck. She ran to a palm tree and began to rub her hands on it.

"A palm tree! I can't believe it. I've seen them on TV, but they're so beautiful! I love this tree! Have you ever seen a palm tree before, GW?"

"Yes, I have. I've traveled quite a bit, Roberta."

"Where did you see them before?"

"I've seen palm trees in California and in North Africa."

"How about you, Mom? Have you ever seen one up close?"

"No, I haven't, Bobbigirl. I'm glad I got to see my first palm tree with you."

"Me too! This is great!"

We stretched our legs for a few minutes and resumed the drive with Ann Marie behind the wheel.

"What do you think, GW? Where should we go?"

"I'm not sure. Let's keep going south. I hear Fort Lauderdale is lovely."

"Is there much building going on around there?"

"I don't know. If you want to go someplace else or stop, I understand. You don't have to keep me with you."

"GW, don't you want to stay with me?" asked Roberta.

"Of course I do, Sweetheart. But you and your mom are going to start a new life here. I might cramp your style somewhat."

"I want you to be part of my new life. You're the best teacher I ever had! Besides, I love you and my mom does too, so you have to stay."

Ann Marie colored a bit and looked straight ahead. "If Bobbigirl says you have to stay, then you have to stay. We can play it by ear and stick together until we get settled. If it's okay with you..."

"I would be delighted."

Ann Marie decided that she'd had enough of secondary roads and brought us to Route 95. We merged back with the fast traffic we left in Rhode Island, and I felt that we had begun something new and exciting.

We stopped at an old fashioned motel, the Palm Grove Motor Court, at the outskirts of Fort Lauderdale. Ann Marie paid for the room due to the fact that she had money from her weeks of working for T-Bone. After eating at a Waffle House, we returned to the room. Roberta appeared to fall asleep watching CNN.

"What do you think we ought to do next, GW?"

"I suggest we find a two bedroom apartment we can afford. Once I have an address, I'll inform the Social Security Administration, and I'll start getting my checks again. Then Roberta can be enrolled in school and we can see about finding work."

"And if we start getting on your nerves, or visa-versa,

we go our own way. No lease, just a week to week or month to month type of place. What do you say?"

"You have yourself a deal, Ann."

We heard Roberta begin to giggle under her blanket.

It had been quite a while since I had gone apartment hunting. We found a two bedroom house with a small scrubby yard in Clearview Lake. A hovel under sunny skies amid palm trees is still a hovel. The outside stucco was chipped and scarred and showed tumors of patchwork repairs. A chain link fence that was held up by vines surrounded the yard of dirt and tufts of grass. The inside was drab and unlovely, but reasonably clean.

"Mommy, this is the nicest place we've ever lived! I love it here. And GW, you're the nicest person we ever lived with."

"Thank you, Roberta. You're the liveliest people I've lived with in a very long time."

"Do I remind you of your daughter when she was a girl?"

"Yes, you do."

"Do I look like her?"

"No, but you make me feel the way she did when she was a girl."

"How is that?"

"Privileged to be in the company of a lovely and unpredictable girl who looks at life as an adventure."

"Life *is* an adventure, isn't it, GW?"

"Only a life well spent."

Roberta looked quite serious and said, "My life's going to be an adventure."

Ann Marie and I took Roberta to Santos Elementary School to register her. We sat with the principal, Mrs. Sanchin, and explained that Roberta had been in second grade, but was far more advanced.

"We don't have any formal program for gifted students

78

here. I suggest that we start her in her own grade, and allow the teacher to give her additional work, and perhaps she can skip a grade down the line."

"Do any public schools in this area have gifted programs?"

"I'm afraid not. There are several schools that cater to problem students, but nothing for the exceptional. Unfortunately the system is skewed toward providing for the bottom rather than the top, or even the middle."

"When can Roberta start?"

"If you have her transcript from Massachusetts, she can begin tomorrow."

"Why can't GW keep teaching me? He's smarter than the teacher I had in Westborough."

"Of course home schooling is always an option. You'll need to know what our second grade curriculum is so that Roberta gets the basics we require as well as anything extra you are able to teach her. Are you going to enroll Roberta here, Ms. Fobbs?"

"Can I take some time to think about it?"

"Not more than one or two days. Florida law requires that all children attend school or receive acceptable home schooling. You need to let the district know if you are going to home school so that Family Services aren't called down on you."

"Then I'll enroll her for now. I can pull her out for home schooling at any time, right?"

"That's right."

Ann filled out the enrollment forms and we left. Roberta dragged her feet and walked with her head down.

"What's wrong, Bobbigirl?" Ann asked when we got outside.

"I want GW to teach me."

Ann looked at me with a question on her face.

"Roberta" I began, "I would love to teach you. The problem is that I really am not qualified to teach you math and sciences. But I have an idea about that. I don't want to say what it is yet in case it doesn't work out, but I should know within a day or two. Will you start school tomorrow and trust me to talk to you and your mother about this in a few days?"

"Will you still read good books with me at night?"

"Of course."

"Okay then. I'll wait."

8. LWCC

I looked myself over carefully in the mirror. The new light-weight suit fit well, the tie was knotted perfectly, and my shoes had a bright shine. I had shaved carefully and close, and combed my hair neatly. My small brown portfolio was empty save for my employment record at Holy Cross, a curriculum vitae, and copies of two of my more recent journal articles; "Shakespeare in Modern Film" and "An Etymological Study of Shakespeare's Tragedies." I was a bit nervous; it had been more than forty years since my last job interview.

The bus brought me to Lake Worth Community College where I had an appointment with the President of the College and Chairman of the English Department. I was accustomed to the hilly urban campus of Holy Cross College in Worcester. Where Holy Cross is dominated by large old brick buildings, LWCC was flat and dominated by palm trees, modern concrete and glass buildings, and outdoor courts of every type. However the students milling about were much like students on campuses all over the country. The snatches of music and conversations, the slouching walk of backpack-toting students felt familiar and comforting.

The secretary for the president only kept me waiting a few minutes. I suppose college presidents feel it unseemly to begin an appointment on time, regardless of the relative reputation of the institution.

"Dr. Hodge, I'm pleased to meet you. My name is Christine Newton. This gentleman is Dr. William S.B.F. Evans, the Chairman of the English Department," she said, gesturing to a fortyish man standing beside her.

I assured them I was pleased to meet them as we settled on leather chairs around the president's desk.

"Dr. Hodge, I am somewhat surprised that a man with your background has applied for a position here," began President Newton. "You know, most semesters we don't offer any Shakespeare seminars. Most of our students didn't do well enough to get into the college of their choice. They put in two years here hoping to transfer to a four year school to earn a bachelor's degree. Many of our students will go no further than their Associates Degree, and others take classes occasionally with no intention of ever obtaining a degree. What would you do here?"

"I would teach. As you suggested, my personal specialty is Shakespeare. Nevertheless, I have taught and am completely able to teach modern English and American Literature courses. I can also teach poetry appreciation courses as well as basic and remedial courses designed to strengthen students' grasp of grammar and spelling. I have taught courses that focus on critical reading of historical articles and recent journalism."

Perhaps tired of being left out of the conversation, Chairman Evans needed to be heard. His accent confirmed that he was not a carpetbagger like myself. Dr. Evans was a Son of The South.

"Dr. Hodge, why return to teaching after five years?

And why at this level?"

"I wish to return to teaching for two simple reasons. I miss it, and I could use the money. I'm new to this area and would prefer to teach at a Junior College where I won't be pressured to publish anymore. I am also too old to be dragged into department politics, and nobody will be threatened by me because I don't see this job as a stepping stone to something else. Teaching willing students is what I want to do. Also, if I teach here, there is a personal request I would like to make, and it is one that is more suitable to this school than a four year school."

"What would that request be?" President Newton asked.

"I am home schooling the daughter of a close family friend. She is seven years old, but is capable of high school level work. I would like her to be able to take classes here without formally enrolling as a student."

"That's it?"

"That's it."

"Can you start by picking up one class now? The woman who taught Expository Writing just moved. She has three classes."

"Does she use a particular text?"

"Just Strunk and White."

"I would be delighted."

That evening at dinner I told Ann and Roberta about my new job.

"What's it pay?"

"The princely sum of two thousand dollars per class per semester. I'm taking over three classes this semester, so I'll get six thousand dollars."

"That's not a heck of a lot of money, GW."

"No, but it's not a heck of a lot of work either. The classes each meet for two hours a week. The preparation time and grading for these classes will not be difficult. There is also a very good fringe benefit to this job. The president of the college agreed that Roberta may take any class. She will take exams and participate and receive a grade, but she will not be officially enrolled."

"Does that mean you can be my teacher, GW?"

"Yes it does, but not just me. You will be able to take classes with any teacher in the school, as long as it's all right with your mother."

"Sure, I think it's great! And I have some good news, too. I'll be tending bar four nights a week at the Sparky's Cue and Brew. That'll leave days free for me to find construction work. So, for at least the short term, our money problems are solved."

Roberta sang out, "I knew this would be great. This is the best family I ever had!"

"Don't get ahead of yourself, Bobbigirl. Everything going on here is temporary."

"Mommy, everything is always temporary."

The next day was sunny and clear as I began the next part of my teaching career. Professor Evans introduced me to the class and sat in the rear to observe. Thankfully, we were in a small classroom rather than a lecture hall. There were only fourteen students in the class. They wore shorts and tee shirts printed with the names of pizza parlors and sports teams.

"Good morning, ladies and gentlemen. My name is George Hodge, and I will be taking over for Professor Feingold. This class is called Expository Writing. Who can tell me what "expository" means?"

Two hands tentatively rose above the bowed heads of the class. I pointed at the man closer to me.

"Your name, sir?"

"Tim West."

"What does "expository" mean, Tim."

"To explain."

"Right. Webster tells us expository means 'of or containing exposition; explanatory.' What do you expect from this class?"

"I'm not sure," Tim mumbled.

"Anyone else? No? Why are you in this class?"

"Because it's a requirement," volunteered a girl in front. The class laughed and I laughed with them.

"This class," I explained, "is intended to help teach you to simply and clearly express your thoughts on paper. Any of you that have followed instructions to put together a bookcase from a kit has experienced firsthand how difficult it can be for some people to write simple instructions. Clarity of thought leads to clear writing."

At the end of the hour, one of the students came to me and thanked me and told me how much she enjoyed the class. As I thanked her, I realized how much I'd loved my career. Doctor Evans joined me as I prepared to leave.

"I enjoyed the class, Dr. Hodge. It's a pleasure to hear a teacher take this class seriously."

"Thank you. And please call me George. So I passed the audition?"

"Without breaking a sweat. And I'd appreciate it if you called me Billy. Even the kids call me Professor Billy. Since you're done for the day, how about joining me for a drink?"

"You want me to call a grown man 'Billy'?"

"George, you are well south of the Mason-Dixon line. I aim to be accommodating, so if it makes you feel better, you can call me Bill, but only my parents have ever been allowed to call me William."

"All right, Billy. Where to?"

"My office is close, if you like Scotch."

We walked through the building to Billy's office, which consisted of a desk, two wing chairs, two bookcases, and piles of papers and books strewn about. The desktop was covered with folders and a high pile of papers weighted down with a brass nameplate reading "W.S.B.F. Evans." He pulled a bottle of Glenlivit and two highball glasses out of a desk drawer and poured with a heavy hand. We touched glasses and Billy toasted to "mediocre education."

"What exactly does W.S.B.F. stand for, Billy?"

"You are now enjoying a slug of good Scotch with William Stonewall Bragg Forrest Evans, a proud scion of the Confederacy. My forebears fought gallantly for the Confederate States of America, and I was named after Generals Stonewall Jackson, Braxton Bragg, Nathaniel Bedford Forrest, and, of course, I bear the last name of great-great grandfather, Sheridan Evans."

"Your family is of a military bent?"

"My brothers and I were fourth generation cadets at The Citadel. It nearly broke my father's heart when I did not choose to become a commissioned officer after graduation. Luckily, my older brothers both did their duty, which I believe lessened the blow of my perfidiousness."

"Are your brothers still in?"

"Both full colonels, one in the army and the other a marine. Now it's your turn. Why are you really here?"

"My wife died this past year after a long illness. I spent our life savings caring for her and managed to lose my house in the process. I have no family, so I decided to come south for a fresh start in warm weather."

"So what's this about home schooling a family friend?"

"I was broke. My intention was to hitchhike to Florida from Massachusetts. My first ride brought me the entire way. A woman named Ann Marie Fobbs and her daughter, Roberta. We became quite close on the way here. I began tutoring Roberta and discovered that she's gifted. None of the schools in this area have programs for her, so I'm home schooling her."

"Where are you living?"

"I'm renting a small house with Ms. Fobbs and her daughter."

"You're some operator, George; I'm impressed."

"Don't be. I consider Ann Marie a dear friend. She considers me a harmless old coot and a cheap tutor.

"Why are you here, Billy?" I asked. "This seems like a nice place, but Lake Worth Community College is hardly a fast track in academia."

"I was on the fast track. I took my doctorate at UVA and had an untenured faculty position at William and Mary. I was being published twice a year in the right journals and life was good. I enjoyed teaching and I loved my students. In fact, I loved one a bit too much. The administration was not amused by a pregnant sophomore."

"I should think not."

"I know there's no excuse to be made, but I loved her. In fact, I asked her to marry me."

"Did you?"

"No. It turned out that she wasn't all that interested in an unemployed teacher fifteen years her senior. She lost the baby and we went our separate ways. The school quietly got rid of me and made sure that I would not land on my feet at a higher echelon school. I learned my lesson; I keep my hands off the students. Now my principle vice is that I drink too much."

"Do you still publish?"

"I stopped submitting years ago. If I'm lucky, TV Guide may accept my work, but scholarly journals are out. The funny thing is I still enjoy what I do. And there's something to be said for being a big fish in a little pond."

"It's a lucky man who enjoys his penance."

"Amen to that, Dr. Hodge."

We finished our drinks and I went home after a day of work.

9. The Past Catches up

While we ate breakfast, Ann Marie told me about her meeting with the school principal to let her know that Roberta was to be home schooled and should not be counted as truant.

"I'm telling you, GW, walking through the school corridors to the principal's office made me feel like I was in trouble. Looking at rows of lockers and kids carrying books, I was fifteen again.When I got to the office, I met with the principal, Ms. Sanchin. I told her that you would be helping tutor Bobbi, and she acted like I was throwing her to the wolves. She said to me, "Excellent. Is Mr. Hodge Roberta's grandfather?"

"Why?" I ask.

Then she said, "Home schooling must be done by a guardian or immediate family member. Which includes parents and grandparents."

"So I asked, what if I want to hire a private tutor? She got huffy and condescending and said, 'An uncertificated teacher is unacceptable. You have a right to school your child as you wish, but you don't have the right to arrange for education by non-professional or sub-standard teachers.' So now I'm getting angry, you know? And I asked her, how she knew that I was not a sub-standard teacher? She said, 'I don't. To tell the truth, in my experience most parents who home school their children do a lousy job.' By that time, my head was spinning and I was trying to keep my temper. I took a deep breath and asked, 'So it's okay if I home school Roberta, no matter how lousy a teacher I am, but I can't hire a tutor who doesn't have teaching credentials in the State of Florida?" The principal then smiled and shook her head and said, 'Exactly!' Does that make sense to you, GW?"

"Not in the least. Is there a problem with me being Roberta's teacher?" I asked.

"No. Because then I asked if great uncles counted as immediate family? If, for instance, George was my father's brother? The principal said, 'Yes, that would be acceptable.' So I told her that George is Roberta's uncle. And that he is also a professor at Lake Worth Community College, so he is a professional teacher. She finally agreed, and then added, "If there are any problems, Roberta can always be re-enrolled here."

"So am I to be Great Uncle George?" I asked Ann Marie.

"Only at Dan Marino Elementary School, or whatever they call that place..."

After that we settled into a routine. On days I didn't go to LWCC, I read with Roberta and discussed books with her. We read fiction, history, newspapers and magazines together. On days I had school, I brought Roberta with me. She took a college remedial math course which was the equivalent of high school algebra. Ann Marie worked evenings at Sparky's Cue and Brew.

Sparky's Cue and Brew is, in my opinion, an unlovely place. It's a squat cinderblock square in the center of a strip mall parking lot. A few scarred brown wood booths frame the entrance. Two pool tables at the center of the room are surrounded by formica tables steadied by matchbook covers under the legs. A large U-shaped bar dominates the back of the room. Televisions hang from metal brackets suspended from the ceiling. Most of the light comes from the televisions and the lights directly over the pool tables, as well as neon signs advertising various brands of beer. The bar caters to a rough trade.

Ann Marie was quite comfortable at work and was admired by her customers. She told me she had no problem brushing off unwanted advances without causing hard feelings or bloodshed, a valuable talent at Sparky's. In the event of trouble, she called one of the bouncers. She described all of the weekend bouncers as being the size of a house. She usually made more than one hundred dollars in tips on weekend evenings and better than fifty dollars on most other nights. A popular sporting event on television would double her tips.

Ann was pulling a Miller draft when she heard a familiar voice.

"Hey barkeep, don't I know you?"

"You better. I lived with your best friend for the better part of a year. How've you been, Shorty?"

"Pretty fair. How you doin' Annie? I haven't seen you since you left Chris. He said you tried to run him over."

"If I tried to run him down, he'd be roadkill. I decided to head south and get a new start. How long you stayin' down here?"

"A week. I'm gonna catch the race at Daytona before I head back."

"How's Chris doing?"

"He's okay. He was really pissed at you for a while, but I guess he cooled down."

"He never cools down that I noticed. Hey, I got drink orders to fill here; say goodbye before you leave."

"You betcha."

Ann Marie told me about meeting with Shorty the next morning and an amazing thing happened to me. I actually felt jealousy! I hadn't been jealous over a woman in decades. I enjoyed feeling angry, silly, and wonderful at the same time.

"Is Shorty likely to tell Mr. Lovett about seeing you?"

"I guess so; those guys are pretty tight. What's bothering you?"

"I don't like the idea of that man knowing where we are. You didn't leave on very good terms. What if he filed criminal charges for trying to run him over? You could face arrest and extradition. Where would that leave Roberta?" To my own ears I sounded convincing.

"What are you going on about, GW? He's not going to the police or anybody else to admit that a chick got the better of him. Is something else bothering you?"

"Forget I mentioned anything."

"If I didn't know better, I'd think you were jealous."

"Please, Ann Marie. I won't dignify that with a response."

"Why wouldn't you be jealous, GW?" asked Roberta who came into the kitchen unnoticed. "Don't you love my mom?"

"Of course I do, Roberta. But not the same way Mr. Lovett did."

"I hope not; he hit her. What's for breakfast?"

Ann Marie prepared French Toast to fortify Roberta for another day of junior college. We rode the bus along Military Path to LWCC. I was having trouble getting used to flat, wide, straight roads after a lifetime in New England. I longed for the narrow roads snaking through the hills of Worcester County. The pine, maple and oak trees that had always pointed skyward for me were replaced by palm trees and occasional fruit trees. There is a homogenous plastic quality to palm trees that I find disconcerting.

Roberta and I would talk about her studies on the bus to LWCC. She read the Diary of Ann Frank, and wanted to talk about World War Two.

"GW, you were alive during World War Two, right?"

"Yes, I was."

"Were you a soldier in the war?"

"Indeed, I was."

"What was it like?"

"It was interesting and sometimes scary. In my case it also involved a lot of walking."

"Where did you go?"

"I was in North Africa, England, Italy, France and Germany. I walked on roads, into deserts, through fields, rivers, snow, and along beaches. We walked through great capital cities, bombed-out cities, small towns and forests."

"Did you have to kill anybody?"

"That isn't something I like to talk about, Roberta. Why do you ask?"

"Because you seem too nice to ever want to hurt anybody."

"I never did want to hurt anybody. Most of us thought of fighting against Adolph Hitler, the ruler of Germany, more than the German soldiers. "

"Did you hate them? The other soldiers, I mean?"

"Not really. I didn't actually know any of the men we fought against. I hated what Nazi Germany stood for, to the extent I even knew."

"You didn't know what they were like?"

"I was a very young man, a boy really, although I didn't think so then. When I joined up, the newspapers were full of stories about the vicious Huns and dirty Japs, and I believed them. As it turned out, the Nazi government truly was evil and had to be stamped out. I'm not sure how the German boys I fought against felt about the Nazis."

"Did you ever meet any of them face to face?"

"Sure. Especially in the final stages of the war. German soldiers were looking for any opportunity to surrender by the end. Some of them were very young, only thirteen or fourteen years old. They knew they were going to lose the war and didn't see any reason to continue fighting a losing battle."

"Did you hate them when you met them?"

"I pitied them. I knew that I would go home to a place that was untouched by war, at least physically. The cities were whole and our families waited for us. Europe wasn't like that. The war was happening over there. Whole cities were bombed into rubble. Civilians as well as soldiers were killed by the thousands. They were going to have to start from scratch."

"What was the worst thing you saw there?"

"I saw a place called Dachau. It was a death camp where the Germans forced people, mostly Jews, to work until they were too weak to work because of hunger and disease. Then, they killed them. When my unit arrived at the camp, whole railroad cars were filled with the rotting corpses of people who were brought to the camp in cattle cars and never let out. Huge pits were filled with thousands of twisted naked bodies. Old and young, men and women, boys and girls. There were huge crematoria where bodies were burned. The prisoners who were left alive were even scarier to see. They looked like walking skeletons. Some of them had a spark of life left in their eyes, and they would survive. Many had eyes that were blank, like a fish in the market. They were already dead, but their bodies didn't know it. Nobody who was there could ever forget the sight or smell of it. That was the worst thing I ever saw."

"When I saw that, I hated the Germans for a little while. But I didn't think that most of the German soldiers I had fought against were like the soldiers at Dachau."

"What did you do when you saw Dachau?"

"I made a decision that I was going to get an education. I wanted to read and study wonderful novels and plays and poems. I was interested in pursuing beauty rather than horror, which was what I felt was the life of a soldier. We traveled the world to put an end to horror and violence, but violence was all around us. I had had enough of it."

We got off the bus and went to class.

When I met Roberta after her math class, she handed me a note from her teacher. It read:

> Dear Prof. Hodge,
> Please come see me this afternoon in my office
> if possible. I would like to talk to you about
> Roberta's progress.
> Sincerely,
> Jimmy Derian

"How did your classes go today, GW?"

"Very well, Roberta. I asked my students to write short descriptions of something in the room and read them to the class. They seemed to enjoy it."

"How many students described you?"

"Three or four dared tread that ground."

"What was your favorite?"

"One young lady described me as a tall, thin distinguished gentleman with untamed white hair, full lips and a strong nose. I'm certain she'll get an A. How was your class?"

"Pretty good."

"Any idea why Professor Derian wants to meet with me?"

"Probably to tell you how wonderful I am."

We walked through the corridors of the math department, past posters of Einstein, Bill Gates and long mathematical proofs. I knocked on Professor Derian's door and entered with permission.

"Good afternoon, Professor Derian, I'm George Hodge. You wanted to see me about Roberta?"

"Yes, Professor Hodge, good of you to come. Could

Roberta wait outside please?"

Roberta looked at me with a half-pleading look, then said, "I'll meet you by the entrance to the building, GW."

I turned to Professor Derian.

"Professor Hodge," he began, you obviously know that Roberta is quite bright. The problem is that I don't know what to do with her."

"Is she disruptive?"

"Not at all. I feel almost as though she's patronizing me. For instance, today the class was working on the quadratic equation."

Mr. Derian began to write an equation on the blackboard. As he wrote, he explained that the quadratic equation is used to solve for X in an equation that looks like this: $ax^2 + bx + c = 0$.

"This is really high school math, but students here need a grounding in Algebra if they plan on transferring to another school that requires calculus."

Pointing at the board, Mr. Derian said, "I put this problem on the board for the class and asked for students to raise their hands when they had an answer."

Writing on the board, he revealed the answer: x equals negative b plus or minus the square root of b squared minus four ac over 2a.

"Roberta raised her hand almost immediately and gave the correct answer. I asked her to write out how she reached the answer. She either would not or could not do it."

"I'm not sure what you're getting at, Mr. Derian. I don't know how you got that answer either. If I ever did know, I've long forgotten."

"That's not the point. Roberta is thinking in terms or processes well beyond what I can teach. She sees a problem like that and knows the correct answer intuitively. It's as if you dropped a coin, and reflexively caught it before it landed. You couldn't tell me exactly what you did or how you did it or even why you did it. You only reacted and achieved your goal because your body and mind worked in absolute unison. That's how Roberta does the math in this class."

"Then you need to teach her to understand the steps and logic that allow her to intuitively reach the correct answer. Make her show you her work."

"I'm afraid I'm wasting her time."

"You're not, Mr. Derian. Roberta is gifted, but she needs to be able to break down the reasons she can do what she does. I would appreciate it if you would allow her to stay in your class. She also needs to learn what she knows, and what she does not know. She is obviously quite bright, but still a young girl. Her intellect is well beyond her maturity."

Professor Derian sighed and agreed to allow Roberta to continue in the course.

I thanked him and went to find Roberta. She was sitting on the front steps reading her math text book.

"Let's go, Roberta."

"So, what did Mr. Derian say? Did he tell you how wonderful I am?"

"Yes, he did. He also told me you have trouble explaining *how* you solve the problems he gives you."

"What's the difference? As long as I get the right answer, why should the way I get it matter? I usually just look at the problem he gives me and I see the answer in my head."

"The way we accomplish our goals in life always matters, Roberta. Even in Algebra."

10. Harmless Chester's

*T*hat evening I planned to join William Evans for a night out with some of his friends. It had been years since I'd gone "out with the boys" and I was looking forward to it. Ann Marie chided me not to go home with any loose women. At 8:00 o'clock, William rang the bell and Roberta answered the door.

"Good evening, young lady. Is Mr. George Hodge here?"

"Yes, please come in" said Roberta, in her most polite voice.

I introduced William to Ann Marie and Roberta and noticed his gaze stay a bit too long on Ann Marie. I kissed Roberta goodnight, and we left in William's Corvette.

"I've got to hand it to you, George; you have great taste in women."

"Of course I do. You should have seen my wife, Katherine."

"A looker?"

"You better believe it. Where are we going?"

"To a place called Harmless Chester's. We'll meet some buddies of mine, including a few members of the English Department from work."

"What kind of a place is it?"

"Country music, beer in the bottle, and dancing."

"Will I be over dressed?"

"You may be the only gentleman in a tie, but don't worry about it; anything goes at Harmless Chester's."

I had been in quite a few dives in my younger days, but none of them were quite like Harmless Chester's. It was set at the end of a long, dark, narrow road lined by canals and palm trees heavy with vines. The road ended at a huge parking lot that surrounded an airplane hangar. The hangar had an electric sign across the front of an old whiskered man in cowboy boots and a ten gallon hat. Above the old cowboy glowed a red electric 'Harmless' and below him a blue electric 'Chester's.'

"This used to be a county airport." William explained to me. "Once the airport went in at West Palm, this place quickly ran to ruin. Chester changed the tarmac to a parking lot and the hangar to the biggest bar in the county."

It took a few moments for my eyes to adjust to the darkness inside. A bar with room for more than fifty stools ran the length of the hangar. Behind the bar at least a dozen bartenders practiced their trade. Red leatherette booths circled the outside walls of corrugated metal, which was devoid of paint. On the walls hung a collection of stuffed alligators, license plates, deer horns, road signs, hub caps, liquor advertisements, football jerseys, antique firearms and one forlorn giant moose head. A cat lay on top of the moose head, presumably keeping watch for Harmless Chester. Overhead dozens of ceiling fans spun, some of the blades with baseball caps attached to them. Most of the floor was concrete with occasional drains covered by grates. The center of the hangar had a large wooden dance floor about three inches higher than the concrete floor. Around the dance floor were unmatched tables of different sizes and shapes in roughly concentric circles spiraling toward the outer walls. One outer wall had the long bar, and the others had semi-circular, red leatherette booths that seated twelve.

I followed William to one of the booths where he introduced me to the eight men who were waiting for us.

"Gentlemen, this is George Hodge. He just started working at Lake Worth after retiring as Professor Emeritus from Holy Cross up in Massachusetts. He needed to test his mettle at Academia's most elite institution."

His friends laughed and introduced themselves to me and I shook hands all around.

"Is this your usual Friday night spot?" I asked.

"Oh yeah," answered, Paul Rumspart, a fat man who said he was a lawyer. "This place can be quite entertaining."

A waitress who looked like Daisy Mae showed up at our table to take drink orders. I wondered if the bouncers looked like Lil' Abner. She left with an order for nine Budweisers and one scotch and soda.

"Watch out for George; he's drinking the hard stuff tonight."

"What choice did I have?" I answered. "I didn't expect to be satisfied with the wine list here."

When my comment drew the laugh I was hoping for, I began to relax. The conversation enveloped me. It was the loose, profane and comfortable discourse of men who know each other. I contributed when necessary, but mostly allowed the cloud of masculinity to surround me. It had been quite a while since I enjoyed the company of several men, and I had forgotten the pleasure of easy camaraderie. Because of my age, I was not drawn into any of the good natured rivalries between the men, and was looked on as an impartial, wise, elder who could settle disputes.

"You're crazy, Dick. Dale Earnhardt was the greatest

driver that NASCAR ever saw."

"Dale was good, but Richard Petty is head and shoulders over any driver, anywhere."

"Well, what do you think, George? Earnhardt or Petty?"

"That, gentlemen, turns on a vital question."

"What question?"

"What is a Nascar?"

Nine faces looked at me in disbelief.

"You're kiddin' me, right George?" asked Phil Porter, a Lake Worth police officer.

"I'm afraid not."

"Whoooooeeee! I know you're a yankee and all, but man, you got to get your priorities straight. NASCAR is the National Association for Stock Car Auto Racing. It is the sport of kings." I was informed by Dwight Jansen, a faculty member at JWCC.

"Actually, horse racing is the sport of kings. What's a stock car?"

"What's a stock car?" Jimmy Farrow asked. "There are some serious gaps in your education, Professor. A stock car is an ordinary production model of car regularly manufactured by an auto company. It could be bought from a dealer's stock, like a Camaro, for instance."

"So the NASCAR racers drive cars just like the cars that come off the assembly lines?"

"Of course not! They modify the engines, steering and suspension. They reinforce the cage around the driver. They get rid of stuff like lights and turn signals. They rebuild the whole damn car."

"Then why do they call it a stock car. It sounds like the opposite of a stock car. It ought to be called custom car racing. It could be the North American Association of Customized Propulsion."

"What would they call that, George?"

"The NAACP."

"Now I know he's a Yankee" laughed Dick Hart.

The conversation continued to cross from NASCAR to women to Governor Chiles to women to football to women to work and back to women.

"You boys ought to see George's roommate," William said. "She's one fine looking woman, isn't she George."

"She's splendid," I said.

"How did you two hook up?"

"We both had an immediate need to leave Massachusetts and no idea where to go. She picked me up hitchhiking and we drove here together. We've been sharing expenses ever since."

"You're shittin' me, right George?" asked Peter.

"I assure you, I am not."

"I thought you were a fucking professor?"

"Actually, I'm an English professor."

"You don't approve of profanity, George?"

"You have to understand, I've spent more than forty years in college classrooms. During that time, it was exceedingly rare to hear a curse unless it was quoted from literature."

"How would Shakespear have said it?" Peter asked.

"He may have called me a knot-pated agatering, puke-stockinged professor."

"That does have a nice ring to it," agreed Peter.

"I'll drink to that!"

"Here, here!" said Robert. "A toast to the proper use of profanity!"

"To Profanity!" we raised our glasses.

After that I allowed myself to get a bit drunk for the first time in years. I enjoyed the feeling of years peeling away as the alcohol took effect.

William drove me home some hours later. I had trouble with the key and made a racket going in through the front door. Ann Marie woke up and must have thought I was an intruder because she charged out of her room yelling, "Get out; I called the police!"

"It's only me, Ann Marie. Sorry I woke you. I'm afraid I

had a bit too much to drink."

"A bit? Jesus Christ, you're blasted! Do you need help getting to bed?"

"I believe I better stop at the bathroom first. I'm remembering why I don't drink much anymore."

The years that the alcohol stripped away were quickly returning twofold. I felt older than Methuselah falling to my knees before the toilet. In the back of my mind I hoped I would not choose that moment to die and leave an embarrassing obituary. Ann Marie helped to clean me up and get me into my bed without shoes or pants. On her way out of my room she could no longer contain herself.

"GW, what were you thinking?"

"I'm afraid I stopped thinking several scotches ago."

"Well, think about this. I've already lived with drunks, and it's a mistake I'm not going to make again." Her sentence was punctuated by a slamming door.

11. Vengeance

*A*nn Marie burst through the door. "Great news! I got a construction job!"

"That's wonderful! Are you going to quit the Cue and Brew?" I asked.

"I'll just cut down for now, to make sure this job will last. But you'll never believe how I got the job! I was driving past a construction site and saw a 'Men Wanted' sign. I met the foreman, a guy named Willie Joe, and he asked me where I last worked. I told him it was outside of Gregoryville, South Carolina, and he asked me, "Who'd you work for?" "Gristle Construction," I told him, and he asked, "Which Gristle?" I told him T-Bone, and he started to laugh and pulled his cell phone out of his pocket and called T-Bone, right then and there. I told him my name and he said into the phone, "Hey T-Bone, it's Willie Joe. Listen, I got a girl here named Ann Marie Fobbs who says she worked for you...That's right...She is? Okay, thanks." Then he looked at me and said, "T-Bone says I better hire you, so I guess I will. Welcome aboard." I start tomorrow, isn't that great?"

"Congratulations Ann Marie. But what about the home schooling for Roberta?"

"You've been doing most of that anyway. She goes to the college when you go. This way I'll be able to eat dinner with you guys and spend the evenings with my Bobbigirl. It's okay with you, isn't it GW?"

"Absolutely!"

Ann Marie hugged me and kissed me on the lips. Then she started dancing around the kitchen with Roberta, so she didn't see me blush.

Roberta said to me, "Isn't this great? I love it when my mom has construction work."

"Why is that?" I asked.

"Because it makes her happy."

Ann Marie insisted on taking us out to dinner to celebrate her good fortune. While we ate she gave me the details as she knew them.

"Thirty bucks an hour plus medical insurance. After six months I get a raise. Willie Joe tells me that with the building boom going on around here, he figures he'll have steady work for at least the next eighteen months to two years. With overtime I should be able to pull in eighty grand a year! Goodbye hamburger helper, hello steak!"

When we arrived home, the front door was ajar. Ann Marie said to me, "I probably just didn't shut it tight, but you wait out here with Bobbigirl while I check it out."

"Why don't we call the police?" I said to her.

"I'll be right back, GW."

Roberta counseled, "Nobody changes mom's mind once it's made up."

"Come on in, the place is empty," Ann Marie yelled.

Ann Marie was getting Roberta ready for bed and I opened the refrigerator to get a glass of juice. There was a handwritten note inside the refrigerator.

Dear Annie,

Sorry I missed you. I guess I'll have to catch you later.

Bye for now.

I showed the note to Ann Marie when she came back into the kitchen. She turned ashen and then her face darkened.

"Goddammit! If that son of a bitch comes back here, I'll kick his ass!"

"The note is unsigned," I pointed out.

"I know that writing. It's Christian Lovett. Shorty must have told him he ran into me."

"Did you give Shorty your address?"

"No. Lovett may be dumb, but he knows how to call for directory assistance."

"Let's call the police." I said.

"No. What are they going to do? The note is unsigned. We don't have proof. And what if we did? He could just say he stopped by, the door was open, so he left a note. If we do that, he'll know he got to me. I won't give him that power over me. Christian is weak. If he doesn't have a clear advantage, he won't try something. He'll probably go away. Plus, I still have a restraining order. He wouldn't dare violate the order; he's petrified of prison."

"Are you sure, Ann Marie? I don't like the idea of that guy around here."

"He can't afford to hang around here for long."

After Roberta went to bed, Ann Marie called Christian Lovett Carpentry. The answering machine informed, "You have reached Christian Lovett Carpentry. I am not available to take your call right now. Please leave a detailed message at the tone, and I will return your call as soon as possible. Your business is important to me."

"See," Ann Marie said. "He hasn't abandoned his business. We don't have to worry about him."

The next morning, Ann Marie started working for

Willie Joe. She was out of the house by 6:00 o'clock. That left Roberta and me to have a leisurely breakfast and head over to LWCC. Coming home, Roberta and I had to jump away from the curb after leaving the bus to avoid a van that nearly hit us.

"I think he did that on purpose, GW. We should report him."

"Why do you think that Roberta? The driver was probably just careless. But we'll keep an eye out for that van."

"Ok, GW."

Ann Marie was already home and cooking when we walked inside.

"Willie Joe has a good bunch of guys working for him. Not a Denny Frick in the bunch. They treated me like everybody else."

"That must be a relief. Are they good workers?"

"They seem to be. I have a good feeling about this job. I brought home a good bottle of wine and dinner fixings to celebrate."

"What about me, Mom?"

"I brought you everything you need for your favorite..."

"Root beer floats?"

"You bet, Bobbigirl."

I washed lettuce and cut tomatoes, carrots and cucumbers while Ann Marie pounded and breaded veal and boiled water for pasta. Roberta stayed in the kitchen with us and read to us from *Of Mice and Men*. Just as we sat down to dinner the door skittered across the kitchen floor after being kicked by Christian Lovett. He was pointing a pistol at us and smiling.

"Ann Marie, how nice to see you again. Aren't you going to invite me in?"

"It's a little late for that. But what I will do is call the cops."

"You can try, but you'll find that the phone is dead."

I picked up the phone, held it to my ear, and nodded to

Ann Marie.

"Who's grandpa?"

"I'm a friend of the family," I answered. "What do you want?"

"I miss our family time together, Ann Marie. Come home with me; it'll be fun."

"The fun was over a long time ago, Chris."

"You smashed up my van and busted up my ankle."

"I don't see how that makes things even for the way you treated me. Now get out and I'll forget this happened. Don't do something you'll regret."

"I've thought this out, Ann Marie. And one thing I won't have is regrets."

Roberta leaped at Christian and he started to laugh. But he stopped laughing when she stabbed him in the thigh with her dinner knife. He howled and Ann Marie and I jumped onto him. We were covered in blood and the gun went off. The refrigerator door had a hole in it. Ann Marie and I froze, and Lovett grabbed Roberta by the hair and held the gun to her head.

"Let her go, Christian. If you hurt her, I'll kill you."

"You're not giving the orders here, Ann Marie. Bobbi and I are going to take a ride...to my place. If the cops show up at my door or try to pull me over, I'll kill her on the spot. Get your phone line fixed, bitch, because I'll be calling you tomorrow to tell you what it's going to cost to get little Bobbi back."

"You know I don't have any money."

"Then you'll just have to get some from your sugar daddy here, otherwise terrible things might just happen."

Ann Marie finally broke down and sobbed. Lovett seemed to feed on that. He smiled and said, "Now that's more like it."

"Mr. Lovett," I said, "If anything happens to Roberta, I will see to it that your death is agonizing."

Christian Lovett was so terrified by my threat that he backhanded me across the face, and then laughed and walked away, pulling Roberta along by the hair. I ran to the door and watched him drive away with Roberta feeling more helpless than at any other time in my life. The van he drove had Florida tags, and I wrote down the number. I put my arms around Ann Marie, and that's how we spent the night.

At first light Ann Marie walked around the house and saw where the phone line had been cut. She repaired it and waited for Lovett to call.

I asked her to call the police. "No. I don't want to risk it. Beside that, who knows what they'll do about me? I disappeared years ago from school and never went back. I haven't always enrolled Bobbigirl in school, so what if they try to take her from me? What if my father tried to get her?"

"That shouldn't matter. The important thing is Roberta's safety."

"I know that, George, but Christian doesn't do well under pressure. If he thinks he's in control, he won't do anything too crazy. But if he's cornered, the jerk would kill Bobbi and go out in a blaze of glory, just so he'd be remembered for *something*. Let's just wait."

We were jolted by the sound of the phone. Ann Marie grabbed it. She held it between us so we were sharing the receiver.

"Hello?"

"Good morning, Annie. I hope you slept well."

"Let me say hello to Bobbi."

We heard rustling over the line and then, "Hello, Mommy."

"Good morning, Bobbigirl. Are you all right, honey?"

"Christian hasn't hurt me, but I'm stuck in a dark room. When . . ."

The next voice was Lovett's. "All right, Annie, now listen: I don't want to hurt Bobbi, but you owe me. After you repay me for the damage to my van, and my ankle, then you can come and pick up Bobbi."

"Where are you?"

"I'm close enough to keep an eye on you, Annie."

"So, what do you want?"

"I want fifteen thousand dollars in cash. That's reasonable, don't you think?"

"How am I supposed to get that kind of money?"

"I don't care how you get it. You don't even have to get it all at once. You can pay me on the installment plan, if you want, Annie. But the sooner I get the money, the quicker you get Bobbi back. And if you call the cops, Bobbi's never going home."

"How do I reach you?"

"You don't. I'll call you every morning, early. And Annie, there's a limit to my patience, so you better get me some cash in the next day or two."

Ann Marie started to ask a question, but we both heard the dial tone. She started to say something to me, but I put a finger to her lips, and said, "She'll be all right, Ann Marie. We'll get the money somehow." Then I motioned for her to follow me outside.

"I don't think we should talk in the house about what we're going to do."

"Why?"

"He broke into our house before he took Roberta. He may have planted a camera or a listening device. He also said that he's close enough to keep an eye on you. We shouldn't take any chances. Inside the house, we'll act like we're going along with him."

"Good idea, GW. All right, listen, we'll get cell phones so we can talk to each other during the day."

"I'll go to work today since I need the money for Babygirl. It'll give me time to think about how I can come up with more money."

"I have one thousand dollars saved; maybe I can borrow a little money from William. Then, when Lovett calls tomorrow, we'll have some money for him. By then, maybe we'll have thought of something more."

Tears began to run down Ann Marie's cheeks. She said, "GW, I don't know what I'd do if you weren't here with me. Thank you."

"I love her too, Ann Marie. We'll get her back."

12. The Cavalry

I went to LWCC and conducted my classes. One of my students was astute enough to inquire if I was feeling all right.

"Absolutely, Susan! I had a bit of trouble sleeping last night. Nothing serious."

"You really don't look well."

As I walked to William's office it occurred to me that in the past none of my students would have dared speak to me in such a familiar manner. Who was changing, me or the students?

I entered William's office, then closed and locked the door behind me. He gave me a quizzical look and waited for me to speak.

"William, I have a problem. But before I tell you about it, I need your word that you can keep a confidence."

He leaned back in his chair and considered me for a moment. "Does it have anything to do with this school?"

"No."

"Then you have my word," he said.

I explained the past relationship between Ann Marie and Christian Lovett as well as the kidnapping. "I would like to borrow one or two thousand dollars for a sort of down payment to this man while we figure out what to do. I can promise you that I'll continue to fill my responsibilities at the college and will pay you back."

"George, I know some people that may be able to help. Let me talk to them."

"Not yet. I have to talk to Ann Marie first. We can't risk anything happening to Roberta."

Robert wrote a check for Fifteen hundred dollars made out to cash, and handed it to me. "This is all I can give you right now without moving some funds around. Take it and let me know what's going on."

"I will. Thank you, William."

Ann Marie was waiting for me at home. We walked into the back yard and she handed me a cell phone.

"I got these for us today. I also got a five-hundred-dollar advance from Willie Joe."

"I got fifteen hundred dollars from William, and another thousand dollars of my own. That gives us twenty five hundred dollars."

"Thirty-five hundred; I have another thousand to kick in from Cue and Brew earnings," she said.

Ann Marie hugged me and thanked me for my support. We went into the house and turned on the television and the radio to interfere with any listening device that Lovett might have planted. Ann Marie and I wordlessly agreed to stay in the same room that night. We were jarred awake by the telephone at three-thirty in the morning.

"Good morning, Annie. I hope I didn't wake you."

"Let me speak to Bobbi."

"Hi, Mommy. When can I come home? I'm scared."

"I love you, Bobbigirl. Soon."

Lovett's voice cut in. "All right now, how much money have you raised so far?"

"Thirty-five hundred dollars."

"Seems you've have been busy. I'll pick it up from you this morning."

"When?"

"Five."

"Where?"

"I'll meet you at the Publix on Lake Worth Road. Middle of the parking lot."

The phone clicked off.

We quickly got dressed and put the cash in an envelope. Ann Marie drove through the lightening streets of Lake Worth, past strip malls and condominium complexes to the Publix. The parking lot was empty and Ann Marie drove to the center of the lot. Within minutes the same van driven by Christian Lovett pulled next to Ann Marie so the two drivers' doors were within a few inches of each other. Lovett rolled down his window, and Roberta could be seen sitting next to him. Her legs and wrists were taped together and the seat belt harness held her in place. Lovett was holding a gun and it was pointed at Roberta.

"Are you okay, Honey?"

"Yes, but I'm scared, Mommy."

"I know, be brave, you'll be home with me soon."

Ann Marie handed the envelope to Lovett. He quickly counted the cash.

"Good job, Annie. At this rate, you'll have Roberta back in no time. I'm going to leave now and I want you stay where you are for five minutes before you drive off. If I see you're following me, I'll kneecap Bobbi. I'll call you tomorrow."

We watched the van pull onto Lake Worth Road and drive toward Route 95. Ann Marie looked at me and said, "All right, let's recap what we know. First, wherever he is, it has to be within a half hour of here. It's got to be a place where he can keep Bobbi without drawing too much attention, so it's probably a house and not a condo or he wouldn't have enough privacy."

"We also know that Roberta's all right. He probably needs money right now, or he wouldn't be taking it in installments. So he's probably not working down here, which means he probably isn't paying rent. Do you know where he could be?"

Ann Marie thought for a moment. "He has a sister who has a place somewhere around here. She lives up north and rents it out during the winter. Maybe it's empty now and he's using it!"

"Excellent. What is her name?"

Ann Marie's face fell. "I only know that her first name is Betsy—at least that is what Chris calls her. I never met her, but I know she's married. I'm not sure what her last name is."

"At least that's something. I have something else to tell you. When I borrowed the fifteen hundred from William, I told him what is happening. He said that he knows some people who might be able to help, but he would have to tell them why. I told him not to do anything until I talked to you. We know that Roberta is still safe, so maybe we should see how Billy can help, so we can get this over with quickly. I'm afraid that the longer it drags on, the greater the risk that Lovett will harm Roberta."

Ann Marie's eyes glazed over and she shook her head. "Okay. Tell him. But there's something else I'm worried about."

"What?"

"Chris loves to be in control, and he's greedy. If he gets the money quickly, I'm afraid he'll refuse to turn Bobbi over, and he'll just ask for more."

"Then we need help. Maybe we should call the police."

"I have a better idea. Let's call the Gristles."

"Why?"

"T-Bone said if I ever had a problem, I could call him. GW, I got a big problem. If he says he can't help, then we'll call the police. In the meantime, you ask Robert to help us. I can't continue to allow Lovett to call the shots. With a guy like him, we need to take control."

As we drove out of the parking lot, Ann Marie called T-Bone on her cell phone, and I called Edna Gristle on mine. Ann Marie dropped me off at LWCC and I stopped in to see Billy.

"How did things go this morning, George?"

"They seemed to go well. Lovett took the money we had, thirty-five hundred dollars, and he left. Roberta was with him, so at least we know she's all right."

"Did you think about what I said?"

"Yes. If you think the people you know can help, then we're willing to accept. I don't know what I can ever do to repay you, but somehow, I will."

"What's your plan?"

"We don't have one yet, other than to make sure Lovett doesn't hurt Roberta and we get her back safe."

"Look George, I'll talk to my boys and get the money together, but I want in. I think a few of the other guys will too.

"Who are they? Do I know them?

"They're the same guys you met at Harmless Chester's. They all liked you, George, and I think some of them would want to be involved."

"Isn't Phil a policeman?"

"Yes. But I don't think that'll stop him."

"We don't want the police involved."

"Neither will Phil, believe me."

"All right. Why don't you meet us at our house this evening at about eight o'clock. Be careful not to talk about any of this inside the house; we think it might be bugged."

"See you tonight, George. And tell Ann Marie not to worry; we'll have the money."

Shortly before eight o'clock, three cars pulled in front of our house. William and the group from Harmless Chester's got out and waited on the driveway. William and the man I recognized as Officer Phil came to the door.

Phil was carrying a metallic case with a wand attached to a wire coming out of it. William put his finger to his lips, and Phil quietly walked around the house slowly waving the wand over every surface. When he passed the wand over the kitchen light fixture, a red light began to blink. The same thing happened near the wall phone in the kitchen, and under the sofa in front of the television. Phil motioned for us to follow him and we all walked outside to the curb.

"Your instincts were correct, George; there's at least three bugs, two in the Kitchen and one in the living room. I didn't find any others, but it would make sense not to talk about our plans inside the house."

"Thank you, Phil." I said. Then William and I made introductions all around. Phil, Robert and Jimmy drove the cars up the block and walked back in case Lovett was occasionally driving by the house. William handed Ann Marie a small LWCC gym bag with eleven thousand, five hundred dollars in neatly bundled stacks of five hundred dollars each. Twenty-three stacks of twenty-dollar bills in all. Ann Marie tried to squeeze back tears as she she hugged William and each of his friends in turn. I don't recall ever seeing so many grown men blush at one time. We were startled by the sound of a truck horn playing Dixie. The Gristles had arrived.

T-Bone, Pie, Edna, Red, LB and Horace got out of a large van that said "Gristle Construction" on the side. Ann Marie ran over and hugged them all, comforted by the presence of family in a trying time. "I can't believe you guys dropped everything to come down here. You're the best!"

"That's what friends do, Annie," Edna said. William's friends stared in awe at the size of the Gristles.

Jimmy whispered to Phil, "I never seen anybody as big as that guy," pointing at Horace.

"I don't think my handcuffs would fit him."

Horace squinted at Phil and said, "I thought there

weren't going to be any police, Annie."

"He's a friend, Horace. He's not here in an official capacity."

"Hey, Horace," yelled LB, "Why don't you show Mr. Policeman what you do with handcuffs?"

"You got a pair with you?" asked Horace.

In answer, Phil pulled a pair of cuffs out of a jacket pocket. Horace stood with his back to Phil and his hands behind his back. "Go ahead officer, cuff me."

Phil went to snap the cuffs on Horace. They wouldn't fit at first, but he squeezed them onto Horace's wrists and managed to close them. Horace's hands immediately began to turn purple. Horace turned to face Phil. "That's a good job, Officer; most can't get them on me. Let me shake your hand." Horace pulled his hands apart and reached forward to shake Phil's hand. The broken chain dangled from each manacle. The Gristles all laughed and after a moment, so did Phil. He got out the key and unlocked the manacles from Horace's wrists. Horace winked at Phil and said, "I'm sure we'll get along, won't we, Officer."

While the television aired to our empty house, we sat in the back yard and planned how to deal with Lovett.

13. Finding Roberta

*W*hen the phone woke me at three-thirty, I was surprised that I had been asleep at all. Ann Marie picked it up after the first ring and held it between us as before.

"Good morning, Annie. Any progress with the money?"

"I have the rest of it."

"Meet me at Publix at four-fifteen, same place. You give me the money, I'll give you Roberta. If you try anything, Roberta will be a cripple." He hung up before Ann Marie could say anything.

Ann Marie and I quickly took turns in the bathroom with our cell phones to call Robert and the Gristles. We told them the meeting was on for four-fifteen at the same place. Ann Marie got behind the wheel and I held the gym bag on my lap. We drove silently through Lake Worth to the Publix lot.

Lovett's van came into the parking lot and parked driver to driver next to us.

"You have the money, Annie?"

"Right here. Where's Roberta?"

"It occurred to me that if I just hand Roberta over to you, then you'll go to the police. I don't like that idea."

"You know I won't. I just want Bobbi back. You have everything you wanted. You win; just give me my girl back!"

"I don't think so. She's safe. I'm going to start driving and put as much distance between you and me as possible. I'll call you in about seven hours, after I'm out of the state, to tell you where she is."

"No. You bring me to Bobbi now, or you don't get the money. I'll kill you, so help me, I'll do it!"

"Annie, Annie, Annie. I'm the man with the gun," Lovett said as he showed us his pistol. "And if you kill me, you'll never find Bobbi alive. And if you keep pissin' me off, I just might have to take a little more money from you for my troubles. Am I clear?"

Ann Marie looked deflated. She motioned for me to give her the bag of cash. I looked at Lovett and told him, "Some things are worse than death. You can end this by taking us to Roberta now; we'll never call the police."

"Well, well, the corpse speaks. Just looking at you old man and I know some things are worse than death. Give over the cash so Annie and Bobbi don't have to find out what those horrible things are." He took the bag from Ann Marie and said, "You'll hear from me later today. Don't follow me."

We watched his tail lights grow dim on Lake Worth Road. Within a minute my cell phone rang.

"This is Billy. I'm following the van now onto Route 95 North. If he's going back to his sister's house, he'll get off at the next exit. You folks can get on 95 North, and I'll call you with directions."

We pulled out of the parking lot and drove in the direction Lovett had gone. Ann Marie was drumming her hands against the steering wheel. She said, "GW, if anything happens to Bobbi, I want Lovett dead. I'm not interested in police, or trials or anything else. If Bobbi is hurt, he's going to die." After a moment of silence, she asked, "Are you okay with that?"

"Absolutely." And as I said it, I realized that I meant it. I was somewhat shocked, and perhaps a bit giddy at the thought of myself as a geriatric vigilante.

My phone rang again and William's voice came through.

"He got off the highway. It looks like he's heading toward the boys. Take your next exit ramp and bear right at the end. Let the Gristles know."

Ann Marie dialed her phone and Edna Gristle answered.

"Edna, it's Annie. Lovett is heading toward you people. Is everybody ready?"

"We sure are, child. Don't worry."

I looked out the window and watched the road rush past me. I relayed directions from William to Ann Marie and the roads got narrower and the houses further apart. Trees, bushes and walls filled in the space between homes. Sailboat masts could be seen peeking over houses, tied to docks in the canals that ran parallel to the street. Ann Marie pulled behind William's car.

"Where is he?" Ann Marie asked William.

"He pulled into his driveway, several houses up the street. The Gristles' van is at the other end of the street. He'd have to pass either us or them to get out."

Ann Marie's phone rang.

"It's Pie here. We're all ready to go, Annie. Mama is walking over there now and the boys are sitting under the dock by the canal. They should be out of sight of the house."

"Has anybody noticed them?"

"Not that we heard. The only problem was an alligator that swam over to check them out."

"What happened?"

"Horace killed it. You should be able to start heading over there now."

We parked William's car in front of the house across the street from Lovett's house and saw Edna ringing the bell. She was carrying a Bible and yelling to a closed door.

"I know somebody's home; I seen you pull in. I just want a moment of your time, to help save your soul. It's a good investment, sir. Just a few moments to let Jesus into your heart and spare you eternal damnation! I can wait, because I know I'm doing the Lord's work. I have everlasting life, do you? Come talk to me, sir; you won't regret it. Praise to God!"

The door pulled open and Lovett stood there.

"Lady, get lost before I call the cops. I got no time for you holy rollers."

"Don't blaspheme in front of me, young man!" Edna yelled. "And don't take the name of our Lord in vain! Have you lost your senses, boy? Do you seek damnation and hellfire?"

"I'm callin' the cops."

"You call the police!" Edna yelled. "I will face the law, if that's what it takes to spread the word!" she yelled even louder. "I'll gladly give my freedom to help a poor sinner like you!"

Lovett stepped out of the house and closed the door behind him. "All right, lady. You win. I'll listen, but please, just stop yelling."

"Now you're showing some sense. Let's go inside and talk about the Lord."

"No, we can talk out here. My daughter's sleeping, and I don't want to wake her."

"She needs to hear the word as much as you do. Get her up!"

"No. She's sick. Real sick. The doctor said she needs rest."

"That's different. Let's pray for your daughter." Edna held Lovett's hand, and none too gently judging by the expression on his face. "Lord," she began, "please protect this man's daughter from harm. I know you will forgive sinners like us, Lord, so I ask you, forgive this sinner before me for what he has done, forgive me for what I am about to do, and protect young Roberta from harm. Amen!"

Lovett jerked his head up as he realized what he'd heard, and tried to pull his hands from Edna. The door opened behind him and Horace, who had entered through the rear of the house, pulled Lovett inside. We parked our car in Lovett's driveway and quickly went into the house.

Lovett was sitting in a kitchen chair surrounded by Edna, Horace, Pie, Red, T-Bone, Glenn, Charlie and Willie Joe. An alligator with its head twisted in the wrong direction was on the floor by Lovett's feet. Ann Marie walked over to Lovett and spit in his face.

"Where is she, Chris?"

"She's in the bathroom."

"If she's hurt, you'll pray for death, you bastard."

I followed Ann Marie down the hall into a bedroom. There was a small, windowless bathroom off of the bedroom. In the floor of the bathroom, a rectangular piece of the flooring was cut out to expose a two-by-six support beam. A chain was looped around the beam and attached by a padlock. The chain was attached to a leg iron around Roberta's ankle. Her ankle had been rubbed raw by the metal. Roberta's eyes were wide over the silver duct tape wrapped around the lower part of her face. There was a small hole in the duct tape and a glass with a straw on the floor near Roberta.

Ann Marie gently pulled the tape away from Roberta's face and they embraced. Tears rolled down Ann Marie's face.

"I love you so much, Bobbigirl! Don't worry; I won't let anything ever happen to you again."

"I was scared, Mommy. And angry, too. I told Christian that you would find me. You're smarter than him."

Despite myself, I laughed and the tension seemed to flow from the room. Edna used the key she liberated from Lovett and unlocked the chain. Roberta screamed, "Mrs. Gristle!" and gave Edna as much of a hug as her little arms could manage. We walked back to the kitchen. Horace was butchering the alligator on the tile floor. He deftly cut the reptile from throat to anus with cuts down the inner part of each leg. He handled the three hundred pound animal as if he were preparing a roast. He spoke to Lovett while he worked.

"Did it make you feel like a big man, taking a little girl?"

There was a ripping sound as he pulled the thick skin from the alligator.

"That wasn't a rhetorical question, Mr. Lovett. I'd like an answer."

"No, sir, it wasn't anything like that. I was just trying to get what was rightfully mine."

"You think Roberta is rightfully yours?" Horace asked as he began to cut pieces of meat from the carcass. He handed the meat to T-Bone, who was rinsing it in the sink and then setting it aside on a counter.

"Not Bobbi; the money. Annie cost me a lot of money. She ran me over, smashed my van, and stole a bunch of my tools. She practically ruined my business."

Horace regarded Lovett silently, and continued to cut the meat. "He says he had a good reason Ma, but I don't think I believe him. Do you?"

"No, I can't say that I do. How about you, T-Bone? Do you believe him?"

"I think the man's lying, Mama. How about you Willie Joe? Do you think that Mr. Lovett is telling the truth?"

Willie Joe rubbed his chin and seemed to consider the question. "It's tough to say, T-Bone. He looks sincere."

"Then it's clear what has to happen," said William. "There needs to be a trial. The man is entitled to defend himself and speak his piece."

"That's right!" screamed Lovett. "Call the cops. I

deserve a trial."

"We don't need to bother the police about this," offered Pie. "We can have a trial right here. Mr. Hodge is an educated man; he can be the judge. We got enough folks here for a jury. I don't see a need to waste a lot of time with a court trial."

"That's a wonderful idea, son, we'll try him here," agreed Edna.

Lovett was sweating profusely and his skin looked gray. "What are you talking about? I get arrested now. I get to have a lawyer. I got rights!"

Horace put his face an inch from Lovett. "You got the rights we give you, boy. You don't need lawyers or nobody else. You just tell what happened. We're a jury of your peers, and we don't need no lawyer to tell us if we're hearing the truth."

Horace put the alligator meat in the freezer while his brothers turned the living room into a court room. An easy chair was pulled in front of the fireplace to serve as the judge's bench. Two sofas and several dining room chairs ran along one side of the room for the jury. Two kitchen chairs faced the judge's chair, one each for prosecutor and defense. I asked Horace to serve as bailiff, and he stood silently behind Lovett. Ann Marie served as prosecutor.

"Madam Prosecutor," I began, "what are the charges?"

Ann Marie stood up and announced, "The Defendant, Christian Lovett, is charged with kidnapping, assault, and unforgivable inhumanity."

"Mr. Lovett, how do you plead?" I asked.

"This is crazy! I'm not pleading anything, I'm not saying anything, and I'm not taking part in this charade. I'm waiting for the police."

"The court will enter a plea of not guilty on your behalf," I ruled. "Madam Prosecutor, do you wish to open?"

"Yes," said Ann Marie. She faced the jury and paced for a moment to collect her composure. "Ladies and gentlemen of the jury, the facts of this case are as simple as they are horrible. I left Christian Lovett, my ex-boyfriend, because he beat me. I got a restraining order against him and he showed up when I was moving my possessions out of his house. He tried to stop me by blocking the driveway with his van, and then he came at me. I drove my truck right into his van and took off. I thought I wouldn't ever see him again. I came from Massachusetts to Florida to make a new life for my daughter, Roberta, and me.

"I guess it wasn't enough for Christian that he chased me a thousand miles away. It wasn't enough that he beat me in front of my daughter. He had to find me here in Florida and do the one thing that could really hurt me. He took my baby."

She paused a moment and stared at Lovett before continuing. "He broke into my house, he planted bugs to spy on me, he held a gun on me, GW and Bobbi, then he took her. When I paid him the money he asked for, he refused to give her back."

"That's a lie!" Lovett yelled. "I told her I would call her and tell her where Bobbi was and I would have, if you lunatics hadn't stopped me."

"You're out of order, Mr. Lovett," I ruled. "If you have another outburst I will have you restrained by the Court Officer. Do I make myself clear?"

"Yeah."

"I said do I make myself clear?"

"I said yeah."

"Mr. Lovett, I don't care for your tone. I will ask you again, do I make myself clear?"

"Yes, sir!" The reality of the situation registered in his brain as he looked, in turn, at each unsmiling face. He tried to stand but felt Horace's hands on his shoulders pushing him back onto his chair.

"You're really not going to call the cops, are you?"

"No, Mr. Lovett. *This* is your trial. I suggest you tell the truth, for nothing else will do. We are not inclined to grant mercy to liars."

Lovett hung his head and cried quietly. Ann Marie continued, "Finally, when we found Bobbi this morning, she was tied up like a dog and had her mouth taped shut. She never did anything to deserve that." Ann Marie then sat down. I looked over at Lovett.

"Does the defense wish to open?"

"Huh?"

"Do you have anything to say in your defense, Mr. Lovett?"

He stood up and stared at the floor. Christian Lovett seemed suddenly quite small. He began mumbling and speaking toward the floor.

"Speak up, Mr. Lovett."

"Sorry. What I'm saying is that it wasn't always bad between Annie and me. We got to know each other because she was working at a bar I used to go to. We started seeing each other and she and Bobbi moved in with me. I never charged them rent or nothin'. I think maybe I loved her, but I'm not sure. I'm a carpenter and woodworker, and I taught her a lot about that stuff. I showed her how to make the joints for the chest she made for Bobbi.

"Somehow, we stopped getting along. I have a bad temper, and I smacked her one night after drinking too much. But I only did it once, and she left the next day. I swear I only wanted to make sure she wasn't taking any of my stuff when she left. I wasn't going to hurt her. When she smashed my truck, she almost killed me. My ankle was pretty messed up for a while.

"I was mad at her, but I never tried to find her. Then a couple of months later a buddy of mine told me that he'd seen her working down here. Then I started thinking about her. I guess I wanted to turn the tables on her, how she left and all that. She made me feel weak. I wanted to do the same to her.

"I took Roberta, but then I regretted it. But once I'd

done it, I didn't know what to do or how to make it end. I didn't think it out good enough. But I swear, I was going to turn Roberta over to her today. I swear it!"

"I think the man is lyin'," said Horace.

"Why is that, Horace?" I asked.

"Because he didn't pack nothin. He didn't look like he was gettin' ready to leave at all, like he told Annie this morning. The refrigerator is loaded with food and beer. That man wasn't goin' nowhere."

"Yes, I was! I was leaving today, I swear it!"

"That's enough, Mr. Lovett. Ann Marie, do you have any other witnesses?"

"Yes. Roberta Fobbs." Roberta came over from the dining room and stood next to me. Ann Marie knelt in front of her and held her hands. "Baby, I need to know everything that happened to you when Chris took you from me, okay?"

"Okay, Mommy."

"How did he get you here?"

"He put tape over my mouth, and he taped my wrists and ankles together. I was on the floor of the van with a blanket over me. He told me that if I tried to get away, he'd kill me."

"Did he bring you right here?"

"Yes, he did. He brought me right into that bathroom where you found me, and he put me on that leash."

"Were you chained the whole two days you were here?"

"Yes. Even when I had to go to the bathroom."

"Did you eat?"

"I could only drink through a straw, through a hole in the tape."

"What did he give you to drink?"

"Milk and some water."

"Did he ever touch you?"

"No. He just talked to me."

"What did he say?"

"He said that it was time that my mama learned who

was boss. He said that this was your fault, and if something happened to me, I should blame you for not taking care of me."

Ann Marie wiped tears from her eyes.

"I'm sorry, Honey."

"Don't be sorry, Mommy; I knew you'd get me. I love you. You're the best mom in the world."

She kissed her daughter and sat down. I told Roberta that she'd done a good job and that she could go back to the other room if she wished.

"I'll watch, if it's all the same to you. I'm quite interested in how this turns out, you know."

"As you wish, Roberta. Ann Marie, do you have anyone else you wish to call?"

"No. I rest my case."

I turned to Lovett. "Do you have anything to add or say in your defense?"

"Yes, I do. I want to say that I never meant to hurt Bobbi. I wasn't going to ask for more money or keep Bobbi any longer."

The members of the jury formed into a huddle. Sharp whispers could be heard going back and forth, as well as intense gesticulating of hands. Heads bobbed up and down, and occasionally one of the jurors would look over at Lovett. For his part, Lovett sat slumped forward with his head in his hands. Edna Gristle spoke up, "We've reached a verdict, George."

"How do you rule?"

"We find Christian Lovett guilty of all charges."

Lovett leaped up and tried to run, but Horace grabbed him before he could cross the room. Horace pushed Lovett onto his chair and held him down.

"I have no choice but to pass sentence. As kidnapping is a capital crime, Christian Lovett, you are sentenced to die."

"You can't do this to me! I have rights! You can't!" he screamed.

"Mr. Lovett," I said, "you have not yet spoken honestly about your crime. I told you earlier, no mercy would be shown to a liar. If you would like to make an honest statement to this court, now is the time."

We watched Lovett sob, and nobody said a word. Ann Marie put a tape recorder on the floor in front of him. She pressed 'record' and stepped away. Lovett drew a deep breath and began to speak.

"My name is Christian Lovett. I kidnapped Roberta Fobbs from her mother. Ann Marie Fobbs, and held her for fifteen thousand dollars ransom. Annie paid me in two installments over two days. I figured that if I got the fifteen that fast, then maybe I could get more. I figured I'd keep milking her as long as I could, then I'd give Bobbi back to her. I'm sorry."

The Gristles and Robert began to put the furniture back where it had been. Horace got a cooler from his van and loaded in the alligator meat and skin. Phil walked into the house in uniform, cuffed Lovett and took the tape from the tape recorder.

"Christian Lovett," he began, "you have the right to remain silent."

"What? Who are you?"

"I'm asking the questions here. I believe this tape contains an admission of assault and battery, kidnapping and extortion, Mr. Lovett. You are under arrest. You have the right to remain silent. Anything you say may be used against you in a court of law. You have the right to an attorney. If you cannot afford an attorney, one shall be appointed to act on your behalf. Do you understand these rights Mr. Lovett?"

"Yeah, I understand. What about them? Aren't you going to arrest them?"

"Arrest who?" asked Phil. The rest of us continued to place the house in order and take our things with us.

That evening, we met back at our house for a celebration. Edna Gristle took over the kitchen. She made several chickens to accompany various alligator delicacies, and T-Bone barbequed some of the alligator meat on the backyard grill. There were cases of beer and soft drinks.

A few hours into the festivities, Phil showed up. We gathered around him to find out what had happened with Lovett. Phil got a plate of barbeque and a long neck bottle of beer, and sat at a small table. He enjoyed telling his story.

"Christian Lovett started screaming that he was set up and that he'd get a lawyer to put us all away. I let him yell for a minute or two and said, 'Okay, if that's what you want, I'll bring you in now and you can try your luck.' So he says, 'Whattaya mean? Is there another option?'

"I told him, yes. I was talking to him in my best cracker accent. I've found that that tends to scare the shit out of anyone with a license plate north of Virginia. I told him, 'I don't want to put lil' Roberta through the trauma of testimony, so I'll jus' keep this heeya tape of yo' admission. I'll be makin' several copies to give to people, folks you don't know.' I fixed a nasty look on him and said, 'Listen, kidnapping is a capital offense heeya in Florida. They ain't no statute of limitations. Yankee scum like you will get the hot shot surer than shit. If you want to live, then you'll do what I say."

And he says, 'What do I have to do?'

And I tell him: 'That's easy. First, you get in your truck then you drive out of the state. Then you just keep drivin'. I'll make sure you're followed all the way to the border. If you ever come back to this state, I'll see to it that you're arrested and prosecuted, and you *will* be found guilty! And if you ever again call Ann Marie or Roberta, I'll see to it that you're arrested and prosecuted. Same result—get my meaning? And, of course, if anything untoward ever happens to any of the folks that were here today, I'll see to it that Horace visits you. If that happens, there won't be any of you left to prosecute. I think you understand me, boy?'

"I tell you, that boy was shaking his head so hard I thought he'd get whiplash. He took about five minutes to grab some stuff and he was ready to go. I told him that he'd better not get off 95 for nothing—not till he hit Georgia. I followed him for two hours, and then arranged for a buddy who's a state trooper to follow him. I don't think we'll be hearing from Christian Lovett anytime soon."

Ann Marie was the belle of the ball. Music was playing from a hi-fi, and she danced with everybody. Each man in turn would smile, laugh or blush and, of course, try to trump her earlier partners. Working in bars had taught Ann Marie everything from country line dancing to disco gyrations. Roberta was in high spirits and she danced until she finally curled into a ball and fell asleep on Horace's lap. The big man didn't move for the rest of the night except to occasionally stroke her head.

After eleven o'clock, the Harmless Chester's crowd and Willie Joe filtered out. Edna Gristle slept with Ann Marie, I was able to keep my bed, Roberta slept in Horace's lap and the remaining Gristles found couches and pieces of floor on which to sleep. I was unable to sleep so I went into the kitchen to find a snack. When I opened the refrigerator, Horace said, "Hey professor, since your up, will you grab me something?"

"Of course. What would you like?"

"Just throw some gator on a plate, if there's any left."

I didn't think a 2 A.M. snack of cold alligator would sit well with me. I found a piece of pie and poured a glass of milk for Horace and for myself. I sat down with him and watched Roberta's gentle breathing.

"You look like something is bothering you, professor. What is it?"

"I've never done anything like we did today. The closest I ever came to a felony was hitchhiking on a state highway."

"That boy's lucky we didn't do worse to him. He got

off with a scare."

"We kidnapped him and assaulted him. I'm not sure any of us would go to jail, but I know Phil risked his job."

"So what are you really upset about? That we broke the law or that we didn't do worse?"

"I'm not sure that I *am* upset. I'm amazed by the way I feel. When Lovett was helpless and scared, and I was judging him, I felt good. Better than good—alive and powerful. My entire life up until today tells me that I should feel ashamed, or that I should never have taken part in what we did. But I'm glad we did it."

Horace shook his head and gave me a baleful stare. "So you think you're better than us, is that it? It's no surprise that a bunch of backwoods rednecks like us Gristles would be involved in something like this. But you find it amazing that a lily white college professor like yourself would be dragged into our nasty, brutish world? Do I have that right?"

I physically recoiled at what he said and started to protest. I shook my head no, but without conviction. "You know, I never actually thought about it that way, but you're dead on. I wasn't surprised that most of you were willing to grab Lovett." We sat silently for a few minutes while we ate our snacks. "I didn't realize I was such a snob. I apologize to all of you, Horace. Since we met, you have done nothing but give us hospitality and friendship. Now you've also been my teacher. You Gristles may be the finest people I've ever met."

"Of course we are, professor, but it's nice that you're honest enough to take a tough look at yourself. There's hope for you yet."

I tilted my glass of milk in a silent toast to Horace, finished it, and went to bed.

14. Horace Stays

I awoke to the smell of Edna Gristle's cooking. Ann Marie was indulging in scrambled eggs at Edna's insistence, all the while protesting that she would be late to work.

"Willie Joe was there for me, so I've got to be there for him."

Red, Pie, LB, Horace and T-Bone finished eating and moved their conversation to the other room. Roberta didn't stray far from Horace's side. She did come over to give me a good morning kiss, which let me know all was right with the world. Then she followed Horace to help the Gristles pack up their van.

"Sit down, George; there's plenty of breakfast to be had."

"Thank you, Edna. Will you join me?"

"I already ate, but I'll sit with you. How have you been since you left us?"

I warmed my hands on my coffee mug and considered Edna's question. "Until Lovett showed up, things were going well. I found a job teaching young people, which is what I love to do. Roberta has been getting some schooling, and Ann Marie found a job she likes. I only hope that this won't be too traumatic for Roberta."

"People are naturally resilient, George. It's only when we treat them like China dolls that they crack."

"You're probably right. I just hate to think about what she went through."

"Try to protect kids from life and what's left? Living means hurting too. What's so great about joy or love if you can't contrast it with misery and hate? I've watched my boys jump off roofs, fight, and make mistakes I could have told them to avoid. But I've also seen them do wonderful things I could not have imagined them doing, or told them how to do."

"Easier said than done, isn't it?"

"Not when you consider the alternatives."

"How did you become such a philosopher?"

"Never owned a TV. And I had a big family. You learn a lot that way."

I helped myself to a freshly baked roll and more coffee, and enjoyed the sensations of eating good food.

"Are you folks leaving today?" I asked.

"Most of us are... But if it's all right with you and Annie, Horace wants to stick around for a few days. Bobbi's clinging to him like a vine."

"It's fine with me. And I'm sure Ann Marie will be grateful. How will he get home?"

"Don't worry about Horace, he always finds his way home."

I helped Edna clean the kitchen, and enjoyed the company of a contemporary. There are certain universal experiences shared by people one's own age that don't have to be explained or even mentioned. It's a feeling as comfortable as old shoes. After we finished in the kitchen, Roberta and I said goodbye once again to the Gristles.

"Mrs. Gristle, do you think there's such a thing as a

guardian angel?" asked Roberta.

"I'm not entirely sure, Bobbi, but I think there may be guardian angels for people who deserve them. What do you think, Pie?"

"Oh, I know there're guardian angels. But they can only help if somebody's willing to ask for it."

"That's right," agreed T-Bone. "It's always a good idea to know who your guardian angels are so you can keep their number on speed dial."

Roberta hugged and kissed each of the Gristles in turn. Horace whispered a few words to his mother and brothers and then they pulled away. Roberta held Horace's hand and waved goodbye to the others.

"What is there to do in these parts?" Horace asked Roberta.

"I usually go to school. GW comes with me on the bus."

"Then let's go to school. I haven't been to school in a while, so I hope I remember my ABCs."

"That's silly. You can't forget the alphabet! If you have any questions, you can just ask me or GW. We'll help you."

"Do you two go to the same classes?"

"No, he's over in the English Department. I start out in math."

"What kind of math?"

"Mostly algebra, and some other stuff."

"That's my favorite. I guess I'll go to class with you, if that's all right."

"You can come with me, but it's not because I'm scared or anything. I just like your company, Horace Gristle."

"Well, I appreciate that, Bobbi. I like your company too."

We caught the late morning bus to bring us to LWCC. I watched the other riders give a wide berth to Horace. Most stole sidelong glances at him. Horace paid no attention and spoke quietly with Roberta, who sat next to him. A woman with a boy who looked to be about four years old got on the bus and sat down directly across from Horace, Roberta and me. The boy stared openly at Horace, who finally asked, "What can I do for you, son?"

"Is that beard real?" asked the boy.

"Give it a tug and find out?"

"Can I?"

"If it's okay with your mama..."

The boy's mother looked stricken. She didn't know what to say or who she might offend. Horace stood up and leaned over toward the boy and said, "Go ahead, give it a tug."

The boy grabbed and pulled for all he was worth. Horace laughed and sat down. The boy giggled and said, "It's real, Mommy! It's real!"

Roberta and I laughed, and the boy's mother looked relieved. We got off the bus a few minutes after that.

"Does it bother you that people stare at you?" I asked him.

"It's only strangers that do that. I'm used to it. I know how I look. I mean, if I saw somebody as big as me, I think I'd stare too. I haven't met anybody my size since I was sixteen."

"Where I come from you couldn't have walked through the neighborhood without being recruited by every local football coach. Did you face much of that when you were in school?"

"I was recruited my freshman year in High School to play ball. I was already bigger than everybody on the varsity squad. But I only played one game."

"Why?"

"I was positioned at offensive guard and defensive end. In the one game I played, I injured four players. By the third quarter, I could see in the eyes of the boys across the line that they were terrified of me. I'd try to block somebody and he'd fly off me before I could actually hit him. Then he'd get up slowly, like I put a real hurtin' on him. I didn't like the way that felt. So I quit the next day."

"Your coach must have been disappointed."

"He said he was, but I think he may have been relieved."

We went our separate ways as Roberta led Horace by the hand to her math class, and I headed to my class.

I faced the group of students who made up my expository writing class. I wrote a single word on the blackboard in large, bold letters: HERO.

"I want you to describe a hero for me. Make it no more than two hundred words. You have ten minutes."

"Does it have to be a famous person, or could it be a family member?" asked an earnest young lady.

"It can be anybody you like, real or imagined. It can be a hero from literature or you could describe the qualities that you think would make the owner of those qualities a hero. Now get cracking, I want to read some of these in class."

Papers shuffled, books were dropped to the floor, and chairs scraped the tiles until the only sounds left in the room were the scratches of pens on paper and the collective breathing of the students. I pretended to grade papers for ten minutes.

"Pens down, and pass your papers forward. I won't read names unless you want me to."

Most students were smiling and a few looked sullen. One of the latter spoke up. "Professor Hodge? How is this supposed to help us learn to write better?"

"You just did a writing exercise, Frank. The key to writing clearly is to think clearly. Hopefully, you were able to marshal your thoughts and write a few insightful paragraphs."

I shuffled the papers to change the order.

"A hero is a person who is willing to risk his or her life to help another person. It could be a police officer, fireman or soldier who does something dangerous, all the while knowing the risk. A person who is too dumb to know about danger isn't a hero for taking a risk. He's just a

137

moron.

"A Hero takes a risk because it is the right thing to do, not for riches or rewards."

I looked up at the class. "Any comments?" Several hands went up. "Yes, Erica?" I asked.

"It's okay as far as it goes, but I think that definition is too limiting."

"How so?"

"Acting heroically can involve something other than taking a risk. A person who gives up something for the sake of a friend can be a hero. Like a woman who gives up a promising career to spend time with her children."

"There's nothing heroic about that. That's no more heroic than going to work to earn a paycheck for your family," said Frank.

"I'll bet it was a guy who wrote the definition Professor Hodge read," answered Erica.

"I won't say who wrote it. If the writer wishes to acknowledge this work, now is the time."

"It's mine," Jon Craft volunteered.

"What do you think about Erica's comment?"

"She makes a decent point, I guess. But that's more along the lines of being a good person. Being heroic requires something over and above what's expected or required."

Erica reddened a bit, but said nothing. I shuffled through the papers to find a contrasting definition.

"In 1938, Jacob Resnick and Moses Resnick tried to leave Nazi Germany. Each had a visa, and each had purchased passage on a ship bound for New York. The Resnick brothers made their way to Hamburg to sail to freedom. When they tried to board the ship, a soldier at the pier demanded a bribe of 150 Marks to allow them to board. They argued that he couldn't do that, couldn't he see they had tickets? The soldier laughed and told them, "If you don't like it, then stay, Jews." They had only 210 Marks between them. The soldier would not budge on the price. Jacob Resnick was the older brother. He gave his money to Moses and told him to go aboard, and that he would take another ship. Jacob died in Auschwitz. Jacob was a hero."

"What do you think class?"

"I think Moses was the hero."

"Why is that, Frank?" I asked.

"It's easier to embrace what you know, even if it's terrible. It takes courage to do something different. If Jacob really wanted to get out, then he could have tried something else."

"Anybody else think that Moses was the hero?"

Natalie Rosen's hand went up. "Why do you think Moses was the hero?"

"Because if he hadn't left, I would not have been born. He was my grandfather."

"Then why did you write that Jacob was the hero."

"Because that's the way the story was always told to me."

"Very good, now we're getting to the heart of the matter. We're force fed tales of heroism from the cradle to the grave. Somewhere along the line, you have to question the precepts that you are taught, determine for yourself if they hold true. You must learn to think critically."

"What do you think constitutes a hero, Professor Hodge?"

"My answer to that question changes all the time. When I was a boy, I thought soldiers were heroes. Having been a soldier, I know that only a few are heroes, but most are ordinary. When I was in school, I thought the great writers and thinkers were heroes: Shakespeare, Plato, Aristotle and the like. Maybe they were heroes, but I suspect that they were only very accomplished writers and thinkers. Most people have the capacity for heroism, given the right situation. Today's coward may be tomorrow's hero, and vice versa."

I met Roberta and Horace outside. They were sitting

under a tree talking with William. They waved to me as I approached and William pointed to a spot on the ground where I was to sit. William was laughing and wiping tears from his eyes.

"Looks like I missed something funny."

"Horace was telling stories about some of the people he's met. He told me about Annie's run-in with Donnie Frick. I'll have to remember to be polite to her."

"I was telling Horace that the guys are going to Harmless Chester's tomorrow night. You two ought to come along."

"That'll depend on how Annie and Bobbi feel about being alone," said Horace.

"I told you already, Horace Gristle, Mom and I can take care of ourselves."

"If that's really how you feel, then we'll be kicking up our heels at Harmless Chester's."

True to her word, the next evening Roberta informed her mother that there was no reason Horace had to stay and keep watch over them. William's Corvette was out of the question, so he drove to our house and then we switched to Ann Marie's truck. Without heavy duty suspension, the truck leaned toward the passenger side where Horace sat. William claimed he could barely make a left turn because of the weight distribution. I knew better than to wear a tie for my second trip to Harmless Chester's, and Horace's bib overalls fit the dress code perfectly.

Inside, Horace walked through a sea of ogling faces. Bouncers walked past him in groups of three or more, still keeping their distance. Phil welcomed us to the table and introduced Horace to the boys.

"What do you do, Horace?" Mike the CPA wanted to know.

"Sometimes I work with my brothers doing construction or farm work. But I also freelance to help pay the bills."

"What kind of freelance work?"

"You might call it...bodyguard work."

"You got a card or something?" pressed Mike.

"I only work for people I know, or who another friend can vouch for."

"That's a bit limiting, isn't it?"

"That's the way I like it."

"What's your hourly rate?"

"It ain't like that. I work more on a sliding scale."

"On what do you base your fee?"

"On what the client can afford."

Mike laughed at that and some of the others did too. As the evening wore on, bouncers stopped walking past our table and patrons stopped staring our way. We were like any other table of laughing, drinking men in the hangar, albeit somewhat older.

Phil pulled a chair next to Horace and told him, "Two rough looking guys have been staring at you for a while now."

"I saw 'em. The taller guy is wearing a muscle shirt, black jeans and fancy cowboy boots. The shorter guy is wearing a Harley T-shirt with blue jeans with a chain hanging from his right front pocket."

"That's them. Should I flash a badge and ask them what they want?"

"They're just trying to figure out if they can take me. Want to make a few bucks?"

"What you have in mind?"

"Tell 'em that I'll bet them a hundred bucks each that I can kick their ass in a one against two fight."

"Can you?"

"We can take some side bets and make this interesting."

"How do you know anybody will bet against you?"

Horace got up and dropped his beer mug on the floor. "Sorry, fellas" he boomed. "Gotta go take a squirt." He staggered unsteadily across the floor toward the

141

bathrooms, occasionally bumping into people and slurring an apology. All eyes were on Horace when he stopped and pointed at the two men he had described to Phil. He glared at them. Then he continued his unsteady walk across the dance floor.

Phil walked up to the two men. From our table I could see the three of them gesturing angrily. Phil waved me over and I reluctantly walked to their table.

"This is George. He'll hold the money," Phil said.

"Fine. I guess he's too old to run very far," the tall man said.

Phil counted out two hundred dollars and handed it to me. Each of the other men gave me a hundred.

"We'll see you in the far corner of the parking lot in an hour," Phil said. "If you don't show up, we'll keep the money."

A small crowd began to gather around us, and they were getting excited.

"The big guy is going to fight both Garcia Brothers at the same time?"

"That's right, smart man."

There were screams from the dance floor as Horace fell, scattering people around him. He rose unsteadily to his feet and let out a titanic belch.

"'Excuse me, folks," he said as he wobbled toward our table.

"The Garcias will kill that drunken old farmer. I'll take a hundred bucks of that action."

"You heard the man, George," Phil said. "Take his money and get his name."

After that, the bets came pouring in. Phil took the bets and handed the money to me. Mike wrote down the bettors names and the amount of each bet. He kept a running total in his head. When the total hit fifteen thousand dollars, he announced that the betting was closed because we couldn't cover any more.

The crowd moved outside and several of the bouncers

came along. Horace walked with none of the clumsiness he'd displayed only minutes earlier. The crowd formed a large circle around him and the Garcias. Phil stepped to the center and spoke loud enough for everyone to hear.

"We've got one rule. No weapons! If I see any guns or blades come out, then I'll shoot the son of a bitch. Any objections?"

All three men shook their heads.

"All right then, mix it up."

The Garcias separated to flank Horace. Horace stepped into the center of the circle and stood on the balls of his feet, knees bent, ready to go. On an unseen signal, the Garcias charged Horace at the same time. Horace stepped into the shorter brother and hit him in the chest with a punch that lifted Ramon off the ground and sent him reeling backward several feet. Pedro, the taller Garcia brother, was peppering Horace with kidney punches that sounded like paddles slapping a side of beef. Horace turned and grabbed Pedro by an armpit and by the seat of his pants and lifted him over his head. He tossed him over the heads of the crowd and into the parking lot.

"You boys still game? Or are we done?"

Ramon answered by charging Horace again. He slipped a punch and hit Horace squarely in the gut with his shoulder. The force of the collision knocked Ramon onto his back. He got to his feet, but his right shoulder was sloped downward at a strange angle. His arm hung limply.

"Looks like you separated your shoulder, son. That was a pretty good shot, but I think you're done."

"I think so, too. Let's go, Pedro."

"No way, brother; I can take this guy."

"No you can't. Leave it alone."

Horace hugged the Garcias. Ramon winced but manfully kept from screaming. Horace gave them their money back and congratulated them on a fight well fought.

"Why are you giving the money back?"

"Because you were brave enough to fight a clean fight.

I made plenty on the betting spectators."

"I've never hit anybody like I hit you. You should be pissin' blood. How did you take those kidney shots without going down?"

"Just good breeding, young man. Don't worry, though; I'll feel them tomorrow."

There was some grumbling among the crowd that the fix was in. One man pulled out a pistol and said he wanted his money back.

"That's just a .22, son," Horace told him.

"So?"

"Gettin' shot with a .22 will just make me itchy and irritated. You don't want to irritate me, do you, boy?"

One of the bouncers grabbed the pistol and started to disperse the crowd. Horace split the money equally among us and we drove home.

"You should get extra for doing the fighting," Robert suggested.

"But if I'd lost, you guys would have had to cover the bets."

"Have you ever lost?"

Horace just laughed.

15. Horace Goes

*W*hen we arrived home, Roberta and Ann Marie were asleep. Roberta had crawled into Ann Marie's bed and was hugging the corner of her mother's pillow. Ann Marie's left arm was draped over her daughter's shoulders. Their breathing was soft and steady and their faces unlined and beautiful. Horace slept on an overstuffed chair and I retreated to my bedroom.

The next evening the four of us were playing Clue at the kitchen table. Horace announced that he would be leaving in the morning.

"Are you sure?" Ann Marie asked.

"You folks don't need me around anymore. It's not that I don't enjoy your company, but I have other things that need tending to."

"I'll miss you, Horace. I'll need your address so I can write you long letters," Roberta said.

"I'll look forward to reading them, Bobbi."

"Are you heading back to Gregoryville?"

"Not directly. There are a few opportunities that I need to pursue first. I expect I'll be home in two or three weeks. What are your plans, professor?"

"I thought that I might ask Roberta to help me find a computer to purchase. There are several language programs that would be good for Roberta, and I would like her to begin to learn how to do research on the Internet. Something I never learned much about, but I'm sure Roberta will be able to teach me."

"Really, GW? We can buy a computer?"

"Absolutely!"

"Isn't that kind of extravagant?" asked Ann Marie.

"I came into some money the other night, and this is how I would like to spend it."

"Came into some money, huh? I think I'd like to hear that story a little later." I felt distinctly uncomfortable under Ann Marie's glare, but Horace guffawed, Roberta giggled and then the tension was gone.

The following morning, after a Gristle-sized breakfast, Horace bid us goodbye.

"Can I give you a lift anywhere? Bus station? Airport?" Ann Marie asked.

"No thanks, Annie. I expect my ride to be here directly. I'm meeting him up the street." He kissed Ann Marie and Roberta goodbye, clapped me on the back, picked up his duffel bag and walked down the street. Roberta stared at him and waved, and just before he disappeared around a corner, Horace turned, waved, and then he was gone.

I enlisted William to come with Roberta and me to look for a computer so I could take advantage of his expertise and further enjoy his company. The electronics store was called Computer Land, and it was as big as an old fashioned department store. There were rows of computers and flickering monitors. Walls of shining packages of CDs, DVDs, boxes of software, laptop

146

computers and still smaller personal computers formed electronic canyons throughout the store. I stared at advertisements for products with names like Internet, Ethernet, LAN Networks, bubble jet, laser jet, ink jet and the like. There were also racks of books designed to teach people how to use all these electronic gizmos and wizardry, the book apparently still mightier than the computer.

Somehow, Roberta seemed to know a lot about computers, peripherals and all manner of electronic paraphernalia. She and Billy discussed the pros and cons of different systems in a language I did not quite grasp. It was like listening to natives speak French. By the time I caught on, they were on to another subject.

"What do you think, Bobbi? Did you use any of the computers at LWCC?" asked Billy.

"The library has computers for any student to use."

"So, what do you think we should get?"

"I think any PC with a Pentium four processor and at least 2 gigs of processor speed."

"You may be right," answered Billy. "What do you think, George?"

"I'll rely on your expertise, William. My idea of a word processor is a Royal typewriter."

We left the store with a new computer, several software programs and a desk on which to put it all. Everything needed assembly to one degree or another, so our afternoon was spent setting up Roberta's room to accommodate the technology needed to accommodate her.

Ann Marie came home and cooked the rest of the alligator we had in the freezer along with some fresh vegetables she picked up on the way home.

"How you feeling, Bobbigirl? You miss Horace?"

"Sure, I miss him, but I feel fine. You really don't have to worry about me. I know what happened was bad, but that doesn't mean I have to be afraid all the time. If you ask me, I think Chris is the one who's afraid."

"I'll bet you're right about that. So, did you get the computer working?"

"I sure did. I went online and did a search at Yahoo. Want to guess what I looked up?"

"Do I get any hints?"

"Nope."

"Do you know, GW?" Ann Marie asked.

"No. I watched while Roberta and William got everything working, and then I read for a while."

"Okay, Bobbigirl, was it a place like Paris or Rome?"

"No, it was a person."

"Was it Justin Timberlake? Or some other Backstreet Boy?"

"Not even close."

"Was it the president?"

"No. One more guess."

"Was it Albert Einstein?"

"No again! I looked up George W. Hodge. Professor Emeritus, retired, College of the Holy Cross, Worcester, Massachusetts."

"Me? Did your search turn up anything?"

"Yes. I found out that you were a professor at Holy Cross for more than forty years, and that you wrote over fifty published articles about different writers, one book about the later works of John Milton, and one novel called, *Maywood Street*."

"You wrote a novel, GW?"

"Oh, yes. It must have sold at least 250 copies. And those were at the Holy Cross book store."

"Why didn't you assign it to your students? That would have helped sales."

"Because I never taught a class in modern American drivel."

"You think I can still get a copy?"

"Absolutely not! It has been out of print for quite a while. Your only hope is that a former student of mine will have a yard sale. You may find one there."

"There was more, GW. I went to the Holy Cross website, and there's a section that is devoted to alumni that rate and reminisce about their former professors. There was quite a bit written about you."

"Now you know the awful truth about me, Roberta; I'm a terrible bore."

"A few of your students thought so. One called you a human sedative. But most of them were pretty nice. I printed some out for you if you want to read them." Roberta pulled a few folded sheets from her back pocket and held them out for me. I snapped the paper open with great fanfare, and reached into my pocket for my reading glasses. After loudly clearing my throat, I began to read aloud.

"'If you have to take an English Lit. class, I recommend Professor Hodge. He was able to clearly explain the dense and boring material adequately enough to avoid much of the reading.' And that, Roberta, is what is known as being damned by faint praise."

"Keep reading, GW, toward the bottom of the page."

"'Professor Hodge's classes engaged me and taught me how to think critically. He did not expect students to regurgitate his opinions, but was at his most interesting when there was a lively discussion with opposing views. His classes were the academic highlights of my time at Holy Cross, and the lessons I learned have served me well in the years since graduation.'" I removed my glasses and wiped my eyes. Roberta and Ann Marie grinned but were gracious enough not to say anything.

16. Why me?

The spring semester drew to a quiet close. Billy arranged for me to teach a few summer classes so I could keep a little money coming in. Roberta accompanied me to campus those days and either went to the library or sat in on my class. On days I didn't teach, we took a bus to the beach or read to each other. Occasionally, Roberta would try to teach me how to use the computer a little better. In the evenings, Ann Marie would make us dinner and we would chat or play Scrabble. It was, for me, idyllic, but I couldn't understand how Ann Marie could endure it. One evening, after Roberta had gone to bed, I asked her, "How long do you think you're going to want me around? You must miss the company of people your age."

"You in a hurry to leave, GW?"

"Not at all. I'm happier than I've been in quite a while. I have a job that makes me feel useful, and I love you and Roberta. I'm just not entirely sure what you get out of this arrangement."

"For a professor you sure are one dumb bunny. Bobbi loves you and you're a great teacher. I love you too, you old goat. You're about the kindest man I've ever met, and you never once tried to get in my pants. Christian Lovett is my age. You think I miss having him around?"

"I love you too, Ann Marie, but not like a wife."

"And I love you because you're the best friend I ever had."

The next morning, William asked me into his office after my class.

"It's a bit early for me to hit the bottle that you keep in your desk," I told him.

"It's not that, George. I have something serious to talk to you about."

"Are you all right? You're not ill are you?"

"No, nothing like that."

"What then?"

"I want to ask Ann Marie out."

"For Christ's sake, Billy, I'm not her father. What makes you think I can either grant or withhold permission?"

"I just want to make sure it wouldn't bother you. I respect you, George, and although I know you enjoy my company, I'm not so sure that you respect me."

I considered that for a moment before answering. "I don't respect the choice you made to have an affair with a student. That, however, was quite a while ago. I've seen the way you approach your job now, and I have no doubt that that is a mistake you wouldn't make again. I can never adequately thank you or repay you for the opportunity you have given me here, and more importantly, what you did for Ann Marie and Roberta. I hold you in the highest regard and consider you one of the closest friends I have ever had."

That evening Ann Marie told me that Billy had asked her out.

"So what do you think, GW? Should I go out with him?"

"I'm considering starting an advice column in the local newspaper. 'Ask George, Advice For The Lovelorn.' Why are you asking me?"

"I'm not, really. I was just curious what you'd say. I already told him he could take me out. From what I've seen, he's pretty cute for an English teacher."

"Young lady, I did not come here to be made sport of!"

"I think you're cute too, GW; you can hang with me," Roberta assured me.

"At least I know I can count on your taste and discrimination, Roberta. Thank you."

Billy picked up Ann Marie at eight o'clock, leaving Roberta in my care. I read while she used the computer. The tapping of the keyboard was relaxing, something like a soft rain. The tapping was interrupted by a sound like a small bell ringing.

"Did that come from the computer?" I asked Roberta.

"Yep. Somebody I.M.'d me."

"What is eye emmed?"

"Instant message. C'mere, I'll show you."

I looked at the screen, and a rectangular box contained the message: You have a message from hotteee66. Will you accept? Roberta clicked the mouse on 'yes' and the message from hotteee66 came on the screen: 'Wanna meet in a chatroom?'

"Who is that person, Roberta?"

"Don't know. I usually ignore the IMs, but since you're here, I checked it out."

"Where is the chatroom?"

Roberta typed: Where?

The answer came back: <u>P-chat4545teen8.</u>

Roberta connected to the chat room and the computer showed a list of names of people participating in the chat. On the left side a name and comment would come up. There were several electronic conversations going on at the same time. The comments of people in the group constantly scrolled.

gigirl: where's the capt.?

slkgy: we should hook up Friday nite. going to jay's?

hotteee66: glad you could meet smartie22 asl?

captusa: c u later gigirl ☺

"I'm smartie22. Hotteee66 wants to know my age, sex and location. What should I tell him?" Roberta asked me.

I suggested a twelve-year-old, seventh grade girl in Boca Raton.

smartie22:12 girl Boca Raton fl- G7

hotteee66: middle skool?

smartie22: yep

hotteee66: im in 9th. Skool sucks!

smartie22: mine's not bad.

hotteee66: u must be good at it. Can u do math?

smartie22: what kind?

hotteee66: algebra

smartie22: e-z

hotteee66: meet me and help me out?

smartie22: where r u?

hottie666: lake worth.

"Do you have any way to know who he really is?" I asked Roberta.

"No, he could be anybody."

"Ask him where he wants to meet you."

smartie22: where?

hotteee66: anywhere u want

smartie22: southside mall at OJs?

hotteee66: when?

smartie22: Friday nite at 7?

hotteee66: How will I know u?

smartie22: blond hair, pink top

hotteee66: c u then

smartie22: g2g

Roberta shut off the Internet program and I asked her what g2g meant.

"It's short for 'got to go.' Why do you want me to meet hottie666, GW?"

"I don't, really. I'm going to tell Officer Phil and see what he thinks we should do about it."

"Why?"

"Parenthood is in some ways quite different in the digital age than it was when my children were young, but in other ways, it hasn't changed much since I was your age. A father's job is to protect his child. That means finding out if somebody is a risk to his child and then doing something about it."

"You're more like a grandfather than a father, GW."

"But I love you like you were my own daughter, Roberta."

"What if hotteee66 is a junior high school kid who needs help with math homework?"

"Then I'll be relieved. Do you have many of those chatroom conversations?"

"No."

"How is it you knew to type g2g?"

Roberta's cheeks colored and I was reminded of catching my Jennie putting on her mother's makeup. Roberta alternately stared at the computer and then at my feet. "I guess sometimes I go online and talk to people."

"You know better than that, Roberta. People pretend to be someone else when protected by anonymity. Who is the man behind the curtain? It could be anybody."

"I'm somebody else too, you know. I'm not some little kid who never had a real home or family when I'm online. Sometimes I'm a college student, or a teenager or a boy. It's fun to be somebody else once in a while instead of girl genius."

"I don't want to see you hurt, Roberta. I can understand that hanging around an old man at a Junior College could cramp your style. You can always go to the public school and meet kids your own age."

"Don't be silly, GW. I couldn't stand to go to class with

kids my own age. I love to go to school with you. I just like to be other people sometimes, you know?"

"We'll talk about this later with your mother. Right now, I need to call Officer Phil. Just promise me that you'll never give your address or phone number to anybody over the computer, and you'll absolutely never meet anybody in person you chat to online. Do you promise?"

"Yes, GW. *I promise!*"

Phil brought a young looking police woman to meet with Ann Marie and myself at our home. The police woman, Officer Erickson, loaded software on Roberta's computer that allowed her to print out the transcript of the chatroom conversation between smartie22 and hottie66. She looked at it for a few minutes and began speaking without preamble.

"Okay, first, I don't like his name. I know the sixes seem pretty obvious as a sign of Satan, but it can be pretty bad. Maybe it's a wiseass kid, maybe it's a sicko, but either way it isn't good. Also, he always gets information about Bobbi before he gives any about himself. He gets her age, sex, grade and town before he offers similar information about himself. That allows him to tailor his answers to be attractive to her. He makes himself nearby, but not exactly local. He makes himself a little bit older, but not old enough to be scary. He asks her for help and that makes her feel good, but what ninth grader is seriously going to ask for help with math homework from a seventh grader? Finally, he lets her pick a place that she's comfortable with and can get to easily. He also asks her how he can recognize her."

"How does he know she'll go alone?" Ann Marie asked.

"He doesn't. He's taking a chance she will. He's got nothing to lose, really. If he asks her to go alone, he may scare her off. If she goes with a friend, he can still check her out and follow her if he wants to. Maybe he can even score two girls."

"What do you think we should do?"

"There's no 'we' at this point," Phil said. "We'll take it from here. Officer Erickson can use herself as a decoy and we'll have other officers around. Chances are, nobody shows up. If it's just a goofy ninth grade kid, we read him the riot act and send him home. If it's an adult, we arrest him."

"We want to be there," Ann Marie told him. "We're raising Bobbi, and we need to know what she's up against these days. I don't need to talk to anybody, I just want to watch."

Phil and Officer Erickson excused themselves to speak privately and they walked into the front yard. We could see Officer Erickson shaking her head from side to side but Phil was speaking forcefully. They walked back in and Officer Erickson spoke.

"I don't like the idea at all," she said, "but Officer Waldman feels that you can handle it. We'll get you Friday."

Phil picked us up at four o'clock on Friday. When we got to the security office at the Southside Mall we met Officer Erickson and several other police officers.

"Hey Jeannie, you're looking good." Phil shouted out.

"Watch it, Phil, or I'll get surveillance on you," she answered.

She was wearing a pair of blue jeans and a sports bra when we got there and another female officer was wrapping an ace bandage around her chest. A small round black wire was sticking out of the top of the ace bandage. She put a pink top on that had embroidered flowers and said 'Girl Power' across the front. When they got done with her she looked like a teenager.

Phil explained what was supposed to happen.

"Officer Erickson is going to walk around the mall for about half an hour, until seven o'clock, and then she'll go get a hamburger and sit at a table in front of OJ's. The other officers here are all going to be in visual contact with Officer Erickson. Officer Erickson is also wired for sound, which I'll be able to hear in this office. I can contact all the other officers using these walkie-talkies that look like cell phones. You're going to stay in the office here with me. Got it?"

Anne Marie and I both agreed. Phil winked at Ann Marie then nodded to Jean Erickson and the other officers, who all then left the security room leaving Annie and I and a mall employee who monitored the mall security system to keep Officer Erickson on the main security monitor. It was amazing to watch Officer Erickson work. She walked in the self-conscious way a teenager does, occasionally snapping her gum or twirling it around a finger.

"I can't believe she isn't a twelve-year-old," Ann Marie said. Jeannie even carried a math text book from the local seventh grade middle school against her chest. She walked into stores filled with teenagers and nobody gave her a second look. After taking a few blouses off a display and holding them up in front of a mirror, one sales clerk told her to buy something or get out of the store. Officer Erickson flashed a one-fingered salute and left.

At a few minutes before seven o'clock, she walked out of OJ's with an order of French fries and a chocolate shake and sat at a table. We watched on the monitor as she was approached by a man wearing loose denim shorts riding low with underwear sticking out of them. The shorts extended almost to his ankles. He was wearing a loose t-shirt with a picture on the front of a thin young man with short blond hair flashing two middle fingers over the name "Eminem."

We could hear him talk to Officer Erickson: "You smartie22?"

"You hotteee66?"

"Yep" he said as he sat down with her at the table.

"You're pretty cute for a math whiz."

"You've got lots of ink for a freshman. What's up with that?"

"I got held back a few times. Like I told ya, math's a killer for me. I hope you can help me out with it."

"I guess so. Sit down, I got my math book."

"Not here. I can't think in a crowd. Let's go back to my house. I brought my car."

"I don't know; my parents wouldn't want me to go."

"You're cool right? I'll bring you back later. What the 'rents' don't know won't hurt 'em."

"Okay, lets go."

Phil called everybody on the radio. "She agreed to go back to his place. Still holding visuals?" asked Phil.

"Roger" they all answered.

On the monitor we could see hotteee66 holding Jean by the bicep with his left hand, and he put his right arm around her too. His attention was solely on her and he didn't notice the four plainclothes officers following at a distance.

"You like to do weed, Smartie22? I got some in my car."

"Cool. Let's spark up" she answered.

They walked to the car and Jean asked, "Where's the pot?"

"Inside the trunk; let's take a look."

They walked to the trunk and opened it. He grabbed Jean and quickly put a handcuff around her left wrist, the other end was fastened inside the trunk. Jean kneed him in the thigh and the four officers immediately pounced on hotteee66. They held him down and one officer put a foot on the back of his neck as Ann Marie, Phil and I got to the car.

Phil looked at the man with a concerned expression.

"What's going on here?" he asked him. "Do you need assistance, sir?" he asked in a thick cracker accent. We could see hotteee66 begin to relax.

"Thank God you're here, Officer. These loonies just jumped me for no reason. I never saw them before!" he said.

"Is that raht? Is this your car, suh?"

"Yeah. They're trying to jack me. You gotta arrest them!"

"Ah see. What's yo name suh?"

"Jimmy Freemont."

"You sure it ain't hotteee66?"

"I don't know what you're talking about."

"Good. Then you won't mind if ah search your car. Ah mean, the trunk's open anyway, raht?" Phil said as he helped him off the ground.

"No problem. Just keep those freaks away from me."

"Hmmm... Seems you've got handcuffs attached to a ring welded into the trunk. You got a ball gag, and a black cotton sack. What's all this for, Mr. Freemont?"

"I don't know nothin' about that stuff. These guys jumped me!"

"Mr. Freemont, I would like you to meet Officer Erickson," Phil said as Jeannie took off her blonde wig. "You're under arrest for attempted kidnapping, rape and indecent assault. You have the right to remain silent; you have the right to an attorney. If you can't afford one, we'll assign you the worst goddamn lawyer in the state of Florida! You understand these rights?"

Hotteee66 began to yell. "This is a set-up! I want a lawyer!"

At that point, Ann Marie had heard enough. She stood in front of Freemont and pinched his face between her thumb and forefinger. He stopped yammering and looked at her. Anne Marie leaned in and whispered in his ear. "The fucking you'll get in prison is worse than anything you had planned for my baby, you sick piece of shit. Get ready to spend the next twenty years of your life sucking dick and shitting blood." Freemont's bladder let go at that point. Phil was laughing, but the officers that had to put him in the car weren't as amused. As they were driving away, Anne Marie began yelling again. "Nobody messes with my girl!"

Phil said, "I almost feel bad for the weasel, but not quite." Phil gave us a ride home in his squad car.

"So what happens now?" I asked.

"Right now Jeannie's booking him. If it gets as far as trial, you might have to testify about what you saw when Bobbi and that guy were talking online. We already know the guy's got a sheet, so he won't be out on bail before trial. He's gone for a long time."

I thanked Phil and he left to go back to the station and help Officer Erickson. I peeked in on Roberta, and Ann Marie was with her, cradling her daughter and stroking her hair.

17. The Date

*W*hen I opened the door for Billy, I was reminded of my daughter's boyfriends coming to pick her up for dates in high school. "Come in, young man. Are you in any of Ann Marie's classes?" I asked.

"Very funny, *old* man. I assure you that my intentions are honorable."

"I'm sorry to hear that," Ann Marie said as she came into the room. "So, how do I look, gentlemen?"

She was wearing a simple white dress that clung to her figure and set off her black hair. She wore no jewelry.

"You look great, Annie."

"What do you think, GW?"

"You look quite splendid. I imagine that Mr. Evans may have trouble focusing on anything but you."

"Don't worry, GW. If he gets feisty, I'll just Denny Frick him."

Ann Marie and I laughed and Billy asked, "What's that supposed to mean?"

"Just hope you don't find out, Billy." I warned as they walked out to his car.

As the car with my nominal boss and the closest thing I had to a child pulled away from the curb, Roberta stuck her head into the kitchen.

"Are they gone?" she asked.

"Yes, they are. What should we do, young lady?"

Roberta opened the refrigerator, found no answers there, and then turned toward me. "I don't know, GW; I'm not in the mood for anything particular."

"Is it because your mother is going on a date?"

"Yeah, but it's also how excited she looked about it. I watched her hold up different dresses, put on makeup, wash it off, change her shoes. She was happy."

"Don't you want her to be happy, Roberta?"

"Of course I do! It's just that my mom isn't good at picking the right guy. Look what Christian did to her, and to me!"

"Billy is a good man, honey. Things may not work out between them, but he would never hurt your mother or you."

"It's not just that, GW. What if he messes up our family? I love you, and I want you around."

"I love you too, Roberta. Let's make a promise; no matter what happens, we will always be family."

She hugged me in response, and I knew I had made a very good deal.

Roberta and I sat in the living room and read, and I noticed she kept staring at me over her book. "Are you having difficulty keeping your eyes off a man as handsome as me, Roberta?"

"No. But you *are* handsome!"

"Of course I am. But what are you trying not to say?"

"Why does mom need somebody else? She loves you already."

I collected my thoughts while putting my book down and slipping my reading glasses off.

"Roberta, adults need companionship from people their own age."

"I know about how babies are made, George. I took biology last semester."

"I'm not talking about how babies are made. I mean romantic love and companionship."

"You're my favorite companion, you know."

"And right now, you're mine. But when I was your mother's age, my favorite companion was my wife, Katherine. I couldn't believe how lucky I was. We loved to hold hands and hug each other. We learned how to talk to each other without words. A look or wink or a smile could tell a story. That kind of companionship fills a person in a way that is special. I was lucky that I found that kind of love, not everybody does. But most people never stop looking. Your mom deserves that. Do you understand that, Roberta?"

"I'll try, GW. I'll do what you always say and keep an open mind."

"And that's why you're so special."

"Good night, GW."

"Good night, Roberta."

I had never been able to sleep well when my daughter was out on a date, and now I was apparently in the same place with Ann Marie. I woke to the sound of tires crunching gravel and peered out the window. I saw Billy kiss her goodnight under the bug light and then walk back to his car after the front door closed. I watched it unfold like the end of scores of my daughter's dates. Unlike those occasions, this time I wished she had asked him inside.

Ann Marie saw me on the living room easy chair as she walked into the house.

"Did you wait up for me, George?" she asked.

"I was reading and must have dozed off. How was the date?"

Ann Marie answered as she kicked off her shoes and

put her earrings and necklace on the kitchen table. "It was more fun than I expected. He took me to dinner at a place called Bayview. I ordered lamb chops and wine and he ordered a filet and a Manhattan, and then I thought we were headed for disaster."

"Disaster? Why? What did he spill?"

"Nothing like that, George. He was just nervous as a schoolboy. Sweat was breaking out on his head and he acted like he'd forgotten how to talk. Finally, I said to him, 'Are you ready to talk yet, Billy? Or do you need to powder your nose?' He started to apologize, which I hate." She then did a passable impression of Billy and said, "Sorry, Ann Marie. I can't believe I'm acting like a nervous kid."

Anne Marie continued the story after I laughed.

"So I said, 'You do go out on dates, don't you? I mean, I hope you're not a virgin,' and then he snapped out of it. He sat up tall and held up his glass like he was about to lead a toast, and he said, 'I may be a virtuous ma'am, but not virginal.' After that, we both loosened up and had a great conversation."

"What did you talk about?"

"Ourselves, mostly. He told me about how he lost his last job and some trouble he'd had. I told him about my choices, and everything that went on with my lost years in New England. It was actually pretty amazing."

"How so?"

"We never judged one another. We each told our stories without making excuses or asking for mercy, and none of it mattered. We were defenseless, and though we both had something to lose, it feels like we both won."

"I'm happy for you. What did you do after dinner?" I asked.

We went to a cool blues club. It was inside a narrow house with a sign over a closed door that said, JR."

"Is everything around here called Junior?" I asked.

"No, it stands for Jungle Room. The house band is called the Rhythm Roosters and they play great blues."

"Does he rate a second date?"

"Sure! I expect to be seeing a lot more of Billy Evans. Well, it's late, George. I'm pretty tired, so I'll just say good night."

"Good night, Ann."

Oh, how my life had changed! Wasn't it only last February that I was in Worcester, caring for my dying wife as my world collapsed around me? I had forgotten how to live. I had focused entirely on loss and had ignored a world brimming with life. I'd convinced myself that being a martyr was noble and important; but martyrs are small, petulant and boring.

I looked about our bungalow from my chair and realized that I was now content. Thinking of Roberta, and her blooming intellect, forced a smile onto my usually reserved visage. Being part of Ann Marie's life, and her newfound success, was as fulfilling as any of my past accomplishments. No longer the fierce, beetle-browed academic, I realized that my Lake Worth students laughed more with me than had decades of Holy Cross alumni. It was shocking to realize that I truly wanted to live!

Ann Marie called from her room to me, "Hey, GW, don't forgot to turn off the porch light."

18. The Morning After

I awoke at six o'clock a.m. as is my habit, and I was into my second cup of coffee and had nearly finished the newspaper before Ann Marie joined me in the kitchen.

"Do you always have to get up so early, GW? Just once I'd like to sleep late on a weekend."

"I wasn't aware that I was reading that loudly. I'll try not to move my lips tomorrow morning; perhaps that will help."

"No, you weren't loud. I just sense that somebody is up and about and I can't stay in bed. Paranoid, I guess."

She poured herself a cup of coffee and took a section of the newspaper. She kept glancing at me over the paper or when she thought I wasn't looking.

"GW, I need to ask you something?"

"Go ahead."

"Are you the over-protective type? I mean, would it bother you if I keep seeing Billy?"

"Anne Marie, you really are like a daughter to me. If

166

you and Billy are happy together, then I'm happy for you both."

"That comes as quite a relief to me. Because, to tell the truth, I really miss," she hesitated and settled on "physical companionship."

"That isn't something my first daughter would ever have shared with me."

"If I can't speak my mind, there's no point in talking."

Roberta walked into the kitchen and lifted the orange juice out of the refrigerator and put it on the counter. She stood on a kitchen chair to reach the cabinet with the juice glasses, and took one down. She sat at the table after putting away the juice and opened the lifestyle section of the paper.

"GW, there's an outdoor art show this morning near the beach. Will you take me?"

"If it's okay with your mother, I would love to take you. Would you like to join us, Ann Marie?" I asked.

"I would. How come you didn't ask me, Bobbigirl?"

"I don't know. I guess I thought you had plans with Billy or something."

"Why would you think that?"

"Billy and mama sitting in a tree, K-I-S-S-I-N-G," she sang. "First comes love, then comes marriage, then comes junior in a baby carriage!"

"I am so glad that the younger generation continues to appreciate the classics," I said. Ann Marie turned her head to hide both a smile and a blush, and then turned to chase her daughter. "You rascal! Wait until I get my hands on you!"

I drank coffee as Ann Marie chased Roberta around the kitchen and living room. Roberta finally tired, allowing Ann Marie to pin her to the floor, lift up her shirt, and make a motor boat noise on her stomach.

"No mom, not a yummy tummy! Pleeeeeeeeeaaaaaaaase!"

Both collapsed on the floor in laughter, each holding

the other, unable to get up.

"That was the most unladylike exhibition I have ever seen. I'm not sure I should be seen in public with either of you. I have my reputation as a teacher of Florida's community college students to consider," I said, as I went to shower and get ready for our day.

We drove the pick-up truck to the beach where a stretch of Oceanview Boulevard was closed to traffic to accommodate the booths occupied by budding artists. Some of the exhibits were prints from well-known artists that were displayed by area galleries and those had all the charm of a Wal-Mart. The more interesting booths were those of unknown artists with varying degrees of talent.

We stopped to see a performance artist who sat on a toilet in a Lucite box reading a newspaper. Her pants were puddled around her ankles, but the *Miami Herald* tastefully covered her midsection. Every once in a while she would turn the page with a loud snap of paper or comment about an article she read. The box had a brass plate attached to it with the title "Bourgeois Librarian." Roberta called to her, "Can I have the comics if you've read them?" The librarian acted as if she didn't hear Roberta, or any of the other comments directed at her.

"What do you think Bobbigirl? Is that art?" her mother asked.

"It could be considered a satire on the failure of most Americans to keep informed as well as the general trend toward looking at television and the Internet as the source of entertainment and information rather than the writings of great thinkers. But I think she's just a crazy lady."

"Me, too. If that's art, I'm the Queen of Sheba."

"Nice to meet you, Your Highness."

We turned to face of a predatory smile upon the large head of a young man wearing a muscle shirt and gym shorts, both stretched to the breaking point. "Perhaps I could show you and your dad some of the galleries in the area? My van is parked just down the street."

"No, thank you," Ann Marie answered. We strolled onward.

"What's wrong? Y'all too good for me?" he yelled as we kept walking.

Roberta held onto her mother's hand and leaned against her hip. She began to shake as tears leaked from the corners of her eyes. Ann Marie knelt in front of her daughter. "Look at me, Roberta. Lift your head and look at me."

Roberta lifted her head as she realized she couldn't hide her tears.

"There are a lot of creeps in the world, and you need to watch yourself, but you can't be afraid all the time. I know you went through a bad time with Chris. That guy that just spoke to us is probably harmless. You have to be careful, but don't let a toad like him ruin your day. Keep your head up—all the time! Do you understand?"

"Yes, Mom."

"Good. Now keep walking."

Roberta walked a bit ahead of us, but never out of sight.

Billy and Ann Marie showed each other new horizons. He brought Ann Marie to book readings and to monster truck shows. Ann Marie took Billy to dance clubs and home improvement shows. Billy even enrolled in a woodworking class offered at LWCC to learn more about carpentry. As Billy and Ann Marie courted, or dated, or did whatever it is that people do now, Roberta and I spent a lot of time together at home.

"GW, do you think Billy loves my mom?" Roberta asked me one evening while we played cribbage.

"That would be a question better directed to Billy," I answered.

"Both my mom and Billy would think I was being nosy and inappropriate," she said, drawing out the last word in a drawl reminiscent of Billy's.

I chuckled and answered, "You're right, he would. To tell the truth, I do think he loves her, and I think your mother loves him as well. And for heaven's sake, please don't tell them we had this conversation. If they knew that I had been gossiping with you, they would think I've lost my wits!"

"GW, stop being silly. I think they're in love too. That's why I'm worried. Things never work out for my mom with men."

"You know, Roberta, this may work out, and it may not, but your mom is a smart, kind woman, and Billy is a nice man. We'll have to see what happens."

"It seems risky!"

"Roberta, love is the riskiest thing there is."

"Then why do it?"

"Because true love is worth the risk."

That evening Billy showed up at the house. He brought beer and chips and suggested that we watch the Braves game. After a few innings, I excused myself and joined Roberta in her room to play Scrabble. We used a minute timer to keep the game moving, and as per our custom, Roberta began.

R   G

14

COBRA

"How are you enjoying your classes, Roberta?"

"I love calculus, but I'm having trouble relating to my Revolutionary War class."

```
                              R        G

                              14       8
```

C O B R A

   A

   S

   T

   E

"What do you mean?"

"There's nobody like me in the reading. I mean, life expectancies were shorter, men were killed in the war, others were at sea for months at a time, so you'd think that there were plenty of single mothers taking care of children, right?"

```
                              R        G

                              14       8

                              +60
```

C O B R A

   A

   S

N I T P I C K

   E

"I suppose so."

"Well, there's no mention of them anywhere. Other than Betsy Ross and Abigail Adams, women might as well have not even existed. And there's nothing written about the way children lived during that time period. Did they work? Farm? Fight in the war? Go to school? None of the reading that I've done mentions them."

R	G
14	8
+60	+8

```
C O B R A
    A
    S
N I T P I C K
    E   O
        D
        A
```

"Why don't you ask your professor about it? Or do some independent research? The Internet should be good for something other than attracting ne'er-do-wells."

	R	G
	14	8
	+60	+8
	+18	

```
C O B R A

    A

    S

N I T P I C K

    E   O

    D E M U R E

    A
```

"Will you help me with it?"

"I would be delighted. But do you suppose that the lifestyle of women and children is likely to be historically significant?"

	R	G
	14	8
	+60	+8
	+18	+86

```
                    E
  C O B R A         L
        A           E
        S           V
  N I T P I C K     A
    E   O           T
      D E M U R E
        A
```

"Why wouldn't it be? You can't consider the Washingtons, Adamses, Jeffersons and the rest in a vacuum. They were products of their time and environment. That includes women and children, not just men."

		R	G
W			
H			
A		14	8
T			
E		+60	+8
V			
E	E	+18	+86
C O B R A	L		
A	E		+104
S	V		
N I T P I C K	A		
E O	T		
D E M U R E			
A			

"I think you should talk to your professor tomorrow and get to work on your research."

"If you don't mind, GW, I think I'd like to start researching now and finish this game later."

"Things are already looking grim for me in this game. I resign."

I retired to my room to read with the noise of Roberta's keyboard and the Atlanta Braves beating the Mets in the background. It's wonderful when a house sounds like a home.

19. Four

Someday I must find out the name of the genius who suggested making a Sunday newspaper larger than the other six days. After I finished two cups of coffee, the Miami Herald front page, metro section, book reviews, and editorials, the house began to stir. I wasn't particularly shocked that Billy was the next person to come into the kitchen.

"Good morning, George. Mind if I take some coffee?"

"Not at all. Did you have a pleasant evening?"

"Best night I've ever had. I don't know whether to laugh, cry or howl. I thought I had an inkling what good sex was like. Turns out I was wrong."

"Billy, if you try to give me details, I'll call Horace Gristle to teach you manners."

"No, no, no. I just mean...I guess I don't know what I mean. I'm flummoxed."

"Really? I've never flummoxed anybody before, Billy. Does it hurt?" asked Ann Marie as she walked into the kitchen. She stood behind Billy's chair and leaned over and kissed the top of his head before getting a coffee mug out of the cabinet and joining us at the table.

"I am finding that my flummoxing is not at all painful. More like a combination of confusing and exciting. I would call it *exfusing* or *confiting*, but George would have me thrown off the faculty."

"You can be assured of that. I will not stand idly by and allow you to mistreat the language in such a manner. Even I, sir, have my limits."

"You're right, we should visit the Gristles," Roberta said from the doorway. "You think we could visit them during summer break? I want to see Mrs. Gristle, Horace and T-Bone and all the cousins again. Those guys are a blast."

"We'll see what I can get for time off, and whether Mrs. Gristle will have us all. Somehow, I don't think she'll mind. But no promises."

"I know, Mom. 'We'll see.'"

Billy began cracking eggs, Roberta dipped the bread, and Ann Marie worked the griddle. Billy and Ann Marie leaned over Roberta's head and kissed each other. They stole glances and shared smiles. In ten minutes the table was covered with French toast, syrup, coffee, orange juice, milk and cereal. Elbows were comfortably bumping, chairs scraping, arms reaching across plates and two or three people were speaking at once.

"My kitchen's roomier; we should try having breakfast there."

"When?" asked Ann Marie.

"Say next Thursday? And then daily for the next fifty years."

"Are you talking about all three of us?" Roberta wanted to know.

"Yes, I am. You three are a set, I would make four."

"What on earth made you bring this up during breakfast, Billy? Didn't it occur to you that I might want to talk about this with you privately first?"

"I told you I was flummoxed. And if I'm going to talk to you first, that implies that you would agree and then speak to Roberta and George next. This seems like a great time saver."

"Wrong answer."

"Of course, what I meant to say is, I apologize. It was very inconsiderate and thoughtless of me to bring this matter up at the table without talking to you about it first."

"Better."

"So, what do you say, Mom? Can I see what his house looks like first? Will I have my own room? How do we know he won't turn into a jerk and kick us out?"

"Excellent question. Billy, how do we know that you won't change your mind? I've had about enough of living in somebody else's house. This place might not be a castle, but it's ours. Bobbi's, GW's and mine. What do you think GW?"

"I've never been a kept man before. Give me some time to think about it, please."

"We can start out at my place and then sell it and buy another place together. That way you know it will be ours and not just mine. I love you, Ann Marie, and I never saw it coming. I love Bobbi like a daughter and I've grown mighty fond of George, too. You've put me out of my right mind and reduced me to begging. I'm pleading with you, Ann Marie. Marry me, live with me, be with me and don't ever leave."

"You can't even propose to me in private? What's wrong with you Billy? I love you too, but I have done too many rash things in my life that have come with steep prices to pay. I want a little time. If you still want to marry me in a week, propose to me again, in private next time, and I'll give you my answer." She walked out of the kitchen, and a few minutes later we heard the water running in the shower.

"Do you think I blew it, George?" he asked me.

"I don't presume to know, Billy. What do you think Roberta?"

"You still have a chance, because when Mom asks me about you, I'm going to say that I like you. I know you're no Christian Lovett, but that doesn't make you Prince Charming either."

"That's quite wise, Roberta," I said.

"Of course it is, GW. I was listening when you told me about Shelly the Turtle."

"Shelly the turtle? I know I've read *Yertle the Turtle*, but who's Shelly?" asked Billy.

"It's good to know you've read at least one American classic. I sometimes despair at your lack of fluency regarding many of our important authors," I answered.

"Listen, George, I could teach a Dr. Seuss seminar at LWCC. The problem would be finding qualified students to fill it."

"As a student at LWCC, I don't think that was very nice, Billy. I may have to re-think what I will say to my mother about you."

Roberta walked out of the kitchen, leaving Billy and me to clean up. Her strategy for avoiding housework was sound and the execution flawless. Billy was preoccupied with worry, which allowed me to finish the newspaper while he washed dishes.

20. The Boardroom

*W*hen Billy asked me to attend a meeting of the Board of Directors, I first demurred.

"I don't want to be involved in any school politics, Billy. I just want to teach."

"It's not the College Board of Trustees, George. It's the Board of Directors for the HCSC."

"HCSC?"

"Harmless Chester's Social Club."

"Oh, then I guess I'm in. What is the chartered purpose of the club?"

"To keep its members from hopelessly fouling up their lives."

As it was early, we drove across the seashell lot to a spot near the doors. In its nearly empty state, the palace was cavernous. Billy and I joined the rest of the social club already seated.

"Gentlemen, thank you for coming to this emergency meeting of the board of directors. I have important business to discuss, and I'm glad you boys could get here on a Sunday," Billy intoned to the men seated around the table. The large scarred oak table was under a wagon wheel turned into a light fixture hanging from the ceiling. As per tradition, since Billy had called the meeting, he paid for the drinks until the issue before the board was resolved.

"Why have you called the meeting, Billy?" asked Phil.

"As you know, I've been seeing George's roommate, Anne Marie Fobbs. I'm crazy about her and I may have messed it up."

"What did you do?" asked Phil.

"I asked her to move in with me and then proposed to her in front of George and her daughter, Bobbi."

"Is that all of it?"

"No. I asked them all to move in with me. Then I begged her. Then I inadvertently insulted her daughter, who, by the way, is probably smarter than any of you crackers."

"So, she said no?"

"No. She told me to think about it for a week and then ask her again, in private."

"That definitely means yes," Jimmy said. "What are you worried about?"

"Did you insult Bobbi before or after she said that?" Phil wanted to know.

"After."

"Then you're screwed. You had a chance, but you blew it."

"Wait a minute!" Jimmy cautioned. "Did you even discuss a pre-nup? Anne Marie's a beauty all right, but you know she's working class. You have to protect yourself, Billy."

"Will you stop being a lawyer for a minute?" Billy pleaded.

"Hell, he ought to stop being a lawyer forever," Phil added.

"Gentlemen, you're not helping me. What do I need to

do to make sure she says yes?"

"Are you sure that's what you want?" asked Dale. "If you really want her to say yes, then why did you call us? You know she'll say yes if you ask her properly and give her a ring. I think you want us to tell you how to get out of it without pissing off George."

"You really think so?"

"Absolutely! I'm a trained psychologist. I listen to this sort of equivocation all the time. You want us to talk you out of marriage, not into marriage. Look at this group for a minute. Between the seven of us we have eighteen marriages. Why would you ask us for marital advice?"

"Who better?" said Peter. "Among us, we've made every mistake that can be made. We've married the wrong girl; we've lost the right girl; we've cheated and been the cuckold; we've gambled; we've drunk; ignored and worried marriages to death. If anybody knows how to doom a marriage, it's us! Now, buy us another round."

Shots were chased with beers as the meeting continued.

"I don't think I want a way out. Anne Marie's the right one. Any of you guys think she isn't?"

"Billy, but what do you really know about her? Her past, I mean. You don't even know Roberta's daddy. She had that crazy ex-boyfriend come through here like a disease. Who else is out there? You don't even know George that well... No offense, George."

"None taken."

"I know George. I checked up on him before he was hired. He's written a fair amount, and I even got a faculty picture from Holy Cross, because I couldn't believe a guy with his credentials would even consider the job he took. Annie's told me a lot about her life, and she hasn't hidden anything. She told me she was a runaway, about her lack of education, and about a few run-ins with the law. She didn't approach me, I approached her."

Phil added, "I think she's on the level. I trust her, and I

don't trust just anybody. I only half-trust most of you."

"Another round!"

Billy looked at the waitress and nodded. More drinks were delivered.

"Billy, just wait a week and propose like she asked you to do. Anne Marie doesn't strike me as a tease. She gave you clear instructions. If you want to marry her, all you have to do is ask. What she was really telling you is to make sure you want to marry her. So, do you?"

"She's smart, sexy, and gorgeous. She's tough when she needs to be and has never tried to use me. I know she has a kid, but that girl is something special too. Most kids either bore me or annoy me. Roberta is different."

"Marry her."

"Marry her."

"Marry her."

"Marry her."

"Marry her."

"Marry her."

"Another round!"

"Billy, I have to ask you," I said. "If children either bore you or annoy you, do you think that perhaps education is the wrong line of work for you?"

"I'm not exactly a kindergarten teacher, George. It's the diaper derby and first eight years or so that I don't like. After that, they're people. And I like people—even young people!"

"Does Ann Marie share that view?"

"I don't know. Why?"

"What if she wants more children?"

The color drained from Billy's face, and then returned in bright crimson. "Boys, the board meeting is back in session. What if she wants kids?"

"Do you want kids?"

"I don't know."

"Then what are we discussing?"

"Meeting adjourned...again."

"Another round!"
"And this time George is buying!"

21. Playing it Cool

Roberta spent the morning in my office entering student grades on the 'Graderite' computer system the college insisted I use to enter student grades. I'd spent far too many years entering grades into a grade book and calculating final averages to learn an entirely new way to record student data. I explained to Billy that I could hardly trust a grading program that celebrated misspelling in its title. Nevertheless, the administration insisted that grades not recorded on Graderite did not exist and no student who took my class would receive credit for the course unless the achievement was noted in Graderite. Gloria Picksell, the director of "information services" tried to teach me to use the program.

"Okay George, first you just double click the picture of a test with an "A" on it."

"Would it be okay if I read the instruction manual first?"

"There's a copy built into the program; you just have to

click on 'help'. But it's a waste of time to read the entire manual; most of the stuff you'll never need. You just want to enter grades. But before you do that, you'll need to weight your categories so the computer can calculate final grades correctly."

"How does one weigh a category?"

"For instance, if test grades are sixty percent of the total grade, then you need to assign test grades as point six. Maybe quiz grades are point two, and class participation is another point two. That adds up to a hundred percent. Then maybe your final is weighed more heavily than other tests, so that could be a separate category or a sub-category inside the test category. Whichever you think is easier. So, what do you want to do?"

"I want to read the manual. On paper. Could I have a copy, please?"

"The only way I could do that would be to print out a copy of the .pdf file, but that would be a huge waste of paper, and that's prohibited by the provost because we're supposed to be a green campus. So, where do you want to start?"

"Gloria, I'm sure you're a lovely woman, but please go away. You're giving me a headache. I'll hire someone to do it for me."

"But it's so easy! Once you try it, you'll love it."

"That's what my mother told me about asparagus seventy years ago. It wasn't true then, and it isn't true now. Please, leave me alone."

Ms. Picksell muttered something about being insulted by a fossil and left my office. A rather unproductive meeting.

I hired Roberta to enter all grades into the system. Where I insisted on reading a manual, as a preliminary step before attempting to open a computer program, Roberta merely looked at the screen and intuitively knew what to do. On the rare occasion that she needed further instruction, she positioned the cursor over a question mark and found the information she required. The college would not hire Roberta due to her age, so I paid her in cash to be my secretary. I was becoming quite a rebel in my dotage.

While I graded papers, Roberta answered the phone with a very professional "Professor Hodge's office, how may I direct your call?" She nodded her head with the receiver stuck between her shoulder and her ear, and said, "I'll see if he's available. Please hold. GW, are you here for Billy?"

"Of course." I picked up the phone. "Hello, Billy. To what do I owe the pleasure?"

"I've been trying to reach you. How did you get your secretary to come in on Sunday? And when did you get a secretary? I don't remember approving that."

"It's Roberta. What's so important, Billy?"

"You hired an eight-year-old?"

"She's underemployed; don't worry about her qualifications."

"I want to talk to you about the Board meeting. What do you think about all that?"

"First, I think you might not want to tell Anne Marie about that discussion."

"Yeah, I know. But George, what do you think about my proposition? If Annie's up for it, would you consider moving in with us?"

"I don't know, Billy. What difference would it make?"

"Because you're her father."

"No, I'm not."

"I mean her spiritual father. She thinks of you as her dad, and she wouldn't ever do anything to hurt you or desert you. If you're against it, it probably won't happen."

"Billy, I appreciate the sentiment, but I believe you're exaggerating my importance. Anne Marie is quite independent. She'll do what's best for her, and for Roberta."

"I guess we'll see. I'll talk to you later, George. Get your grades in."

When I hung up the phone Roberta was staring at me.

"Billy wants you to help him with my mom, doesn't he?"

"Something like that."

"If he was smart, he'd buy me off. I'm the key."

"Anne Marie will certainly consider your feelings in this, but ultimately, she'll make the decision that she thinks makes the most sense."

"But I could probably get a new computer out of Billy if I say I'll put in a good word for him, couldn't I?"

"But would you?"

"Nope. But he doesn't know that. I may have a little bit of fun with him. But you know, I like Billy. He helped you and mom with Lovett, he's nice to her, and I bet he wouldn't ever try to hurt her."

"I don't imagine so. Shall we get back to work, Miss Fobbs?"

"Sure," Roberta giggled.

22. Wedding Bells

*T*he way that Ann Marie told it to me was that Billy had boiled and iced two dozen shrimp for a shrimp cocktail, and he'd made a cocktail sauce of his mother's invention and scoured recipe books for a paella recipe that he thought he could handle. He had confessed to Ann Marie that he considered buying everything prepared and passing it off as his own work, but he knew he'd never get away with it. The price of saffron for the paella was more than a like amount of gold, but that didn't matter. Billy was determined to prepare the perfect meal for Ann Marie.

So after preparing most of the food, laying out cheese, crackers and fruit and decanting a bottle of Cono Sur Pinot Noir, and two bottles of Martin Codax Rioja, Billy had had time to take a shower, and after sweating through his first choice of clothes he had had just enough time for a second shower before the doorbell rang. When he'd opened the door he was wearing lightweight tan pants, topsiders without socks, a blue shirt and blue blazer without a tie. Ann Marie had worn a sleeveless black dress, flat shoes and a string of pearls.

"May I come in or not?" she'd asked as he stared.

"Sorry. I was just admiring the view."

He'd escorted Ann Marie into the living room and put on a jazz playlist from his digital musical device. In my day, I put a slightly scratchy LP on a record player for Kat, but it was the same music. Billy and Ann Marie proceeded to dance and talk and laugh and eat and drink.

"I've never had paella before," she confessed. "I like it."

"Glad you liked it. Want to sit a while before desert?"

"I have some desert plans that you're going to like, Billy," Ann Marie actually admitted to saying. Just then the doorbell had rung, and Billy walked over to open the door. But as he opened the door, it was kicked from the outside and swung into Billy's face, knocking him down. Ann Marie ran to him as Christian Lovett stepped inside and leveled a pistol at them both. Billy ran his tongue over a broken tooth and tasted the blood filling his mouth.

"I wasn't happy about the way I left town last year. You know I don't like to lose, Annie."

"A loser like you should be used to it by now," Anne Marie told him.

Lovett responded by hitting her across the face with the pistol. Blood seemed to explode from her face, but Ann Marie did not fall down. She spat a mouthful of blood into Lovett's face and said, "You hit like a girl." Billy struggled to his feet and tried to stand between Ann Marie and Lovett.

"Don't worry, Annie, there's plenty more coming your way." Lovett put his left arm around Ann Marie's neck and placed the barrel of the pistol against her ribs.

"If you don't want me to shoot Annie, then get your ass on one of them kitchen chairs."

He knocked Ann Marie down and handcuffed her to the drain pipe below the kitchen sink. Then he taped Billy's arms and legs to a kitchen chair and ran tape around his chest to attach him to the chair. When he was finished he taped Ann Marie in the same way and sat them facing each other. Neither allowed so much as a tear to leak from their eyes.

"Watch me beat this pussy boyfriend of yours to death, and then I'll take extra time with you, Annie. Nobody fucks with me. And you can be sure I'm going to do worse to that brat of yours."

Billy lisped, "My friends—I believe you already met them—will hunt you down, Lovett. Whatever you think you're going to do to us won't be anything compared to what they'll do to you. If you drive away now, I won't tell them about this. Otherwise, you're a dead man."

Lovett answered by pistol whipping Billy, knocking him unconscious.

"Jesus, Annie, that boy can't take a punch, can he? Don't worry, he's got time to learn." Billy coughed and some teeth landed on his lap. Blood seeped out of his mouth and dripped off his chin, pooling on his lap. "Your future ain't bright, Annie. Maybe if you apologize, then I'll have a change of heart."

"Fuck you!"

Lovett gave her an open handed slap that was loud enough to bring Billy fully around. He brought his hand up for another when Ann Marie apologized.

"I'm sorry. Billy, I'm so sorry I introduced this coward into your life. Christian, I'm sorry I didn't kill you when I ran you over." As she spoke, the grin on Lovett's face fell as he realized her apology was not meant for him. His face reddened and he prepared to strike Ann Marie again as the front door exploded inward when Horace Gristle hit it running. Christian Lovett turned and fired as Horace hit him. Lovett bounced off a wall and was unconscious when he hit the floor. Behind Horace were Phil, T-Bone and myself. Roberta was home being watched by Edna Gristle. Horace grabbed Lovett by the shoulders and shook him awake. Lovett's eyes were as big as pie plates.

"Boy, we made a big mistake by letting you live last time. Some folks just don't learn. You got anything to say to get yourself right?"

"What do you mean?"

"You know what I mean. Got anything to say?"

It was then that I understood what it meant to see a man actually blubber. "I'm sorry. I wasn't really going to kill them, just scare them, like you scared me! I swear!"

Horace gently cradled Lovett's head in his hands, and then quickly wrung his neck in the same way he had dispatched many a chicken.

Phil cut Ann Marie and Billy loose. They held each other and Billy asked Horace, "How did you know?"

"I have friends hereabouts, and a few more up in Massachusetts. I asked them to keep an eye on this boy and let me know if he was coming this way. Last week I heard that he was in Florida, so Mama and I came to make sure nothing bad happened."

At that point, I noticed that Horace was bleeding. "Horace, I think you've been shot!"

"Professor, I know I've been shot. Mama will take a look at it when we get back to your place. This one feels like a .38, not more than a few inches deep. She'll have it out in no time. Phil, I trust that you'll take care of the details."

"I simply responded to the sound of a gunshot. When I arrived on the scene, Ann Marie and Billy were tied up. Christian Lovett was dead, and a blood trail suggests that an unknown party was injured. Is your DNA on file anywhere that might cause a problem?"

Horace smiled. "I don't even have a social security number. I never go to hospitals, and I've never been arrested. I don't expect problems. Billy, what did the other man look like? The guy who was shot?"

"Uhhh...clean shaven man in his twenties with a shaved head. About five feet, ten inches and one hundred sixty pounds."

"Damn, I hope they don't think that's me!" Horace chuckled. "I'll be on my way home with George to say hi to Bobbi and let Mama patch me up. See you folks later."

Billy and Ann Marie stared at one another as they held each other. "This isn't exactly the way I hoped to propose a second time," said Billy.

"You look sexy with a bloody face."

Ann Marie and Billy insisted on sharing the same ambulance to Lake Worth Samaritan Hospital. A paramedic insisted that it was out of the question until Phil whispered something in his ear. They held hands and smiled. Then they both began to laugh at the gap toothed grin of the other. The EMT squeezed in with them and insisted they at least allow him to check their vitals.

When the ambulance arrived at the hospital they were greeted by the chief of surgery, Dr. Edward Crowley.

"Eddie, you don't usually work emergency. Nice to see you," Billy said in greeting.

"Phil gave me a heads up. Let's get you folks inside and assess the damage."

Dr. Crowley motioned to the assembled team of doctors and nurses and they moved Billy and Ann Marie into a curtained room with well-practiced efficiency.

The following Friday afternoon, Ann Marie and Billy were married in a civil ceremony at Lake Worth Town Hall. I was wearing my best suit, and gave the bride away. Phil, in his dress uniform, was the best man. Roberta wore a simple white dress and stood next to her mother. Horace and Edna stood guard behind the wedding party, and Horace stood quietly while tears ran from his eyes and into his beard where they re-emerged a foot below his chin. The rest of Billy's friends filled the small room. The bride wore a simple white dress, similar to her daughter's, and the groom a lightweight tan suit. Both had matching black eyes and were difficult to understand due to wires holding their jaws closed. The local police thus far had no leads on the mysterious man who shot their attacker, the late unlamented Christian Lovett.

23. And Hodge Makes Four

*B*illy and Ann Marie left town hall for their one evening honeymoon at the Palm Beach Four Seasons. As Roberta and I drove home to our bungalow, she was uncharacteristically quiet.

"Are you caught up on your history reading?" I asked her.

"Same old stuff, government helps the rich and abuses the powerless."

"You may be oversimplifying in the interest of brevity."

"GW? How's a married couple supposed to act?"

"There is no 'supposed to' anymore, Roberta. When I married Kat, the husband was supposed to work to support his family, and the wife was expected to keep a nice home and raise the children. Even then it was more of a Madison Avenue image than reality, but millions of us bought into it."

"I don't think my mom will stop working. She always tells me to make sure that I can take care of myself, no matter what. She says that men just come and go."

"Honey, what's bothering you?"

"Wow GW! You never called me 'honey' before!"

"Really? I never thought about it. Does it bother you?"

"No, it sounded nice. I just thought it was worth noting," she giggled. "Anyway," she continued, "it's just..."

"What's bothering you? You can say it."

"Do you still want to be my teacher and hang out with me now that mom is married to Billy?"

"Of course I want to spend time with you."

"What about school?"

"You're the best student I've ever had, so I don't think I'll let you go so easily."

"I love our family. And this kind of big change might mess up everything. What if they fight or get divorced? Where will you live? How am I going to see you?" Roberta started to cry. "I love you, GW, and I'm afraid you'll be gone." She tried to hold back her tears, which only resulted in several heaving gasps.

"Roberta, I don't know if I'll be living with you, but we're family, and that means forever. I'll still be teaching at LWCC and you'll still be attending. Your new stepfather is still my friend and nominal boss, and your mother is still a very dear friend."

"So you're not going anywhere?"

"No, I'm not."

"Couldn't you just say that?"

"I'm not going anywhere."

"I love you, GW."

"I love you too, Roberta."

On Saturday evening Billy and Ann Marie came home while Roberta and I were reading in the kitchen. They were giggling and snorting but not truly laughing due to the constraints of their injured jaws. Ann Marie hugged Roberta and said, "Come with me Bobbigirl" through semi-clenched teeth. They walked into the back yard and Billy sat across from me in the chair that Roberta had vacated.

He fidgeted a bit, asked me if I was comfortable, poured himself a glass of water and then dribbled half of it down his chin when he tried to drink. I could have asked him what he wanted and put him at ease, but I rather enjoyed his discomfort. It is always easier to negotiate from a position of strength, and I sensed a negotiation was inevitable.

"George," he began, "how happy are you teaching glorified high school English to LWCC's finest?"

"I'm ecstatic, Billy. They remind me of the GI Bill soldiers of fifty years ago. The students may not have the best academic credentials, but at least they know the world doesn't owe them a job, an A and a pat on the back. Most of these students are not unfamiliar with work."

"Yes, true, but..." he stammered.

"Are you firing me, Billy?"

"Don't be absurd. You're the most qualified instructor we've ever had. But I'm wondering if there might not be something more rewarding that you could be doing?"

"For God's sake, spit it out Billy."

"He wants to know if you'll spend more time teaching Bobbi one to one and take a smaller class load at the college," Ann Marie said from behind me.

"As much as I would like that, I don't see how I'll be able to pay the rent somewhere on my own if I'm not working. My Social Security alone is well short of what I need."

"I know," Billy said, finding his voice. "But we would like you to move in with us. The house is plenty big so you can live for next to nothing and bank your government check and use that if you want to move. Beside, you'll still make some dough at the college. Financially, it would make sense for you. The real question is whether you want to do it."

By that time Roberta had joined us. "What do you think, young lady?" I asked her. "Do you want a crusty old college don as your teacher?"

Roberta struck a pose rubbing her chin with her left hand and placing her right hand on her hip. Then she ran to me, hugged my neck and said, "It's settled!"

And so it was.

Due to my advanced age, Ann Marie and Billy insisted that I not lift anything. Roberta simply called me lazy. There was no question of using a mover while Horace and Edna were around. Edna said she was too tired to help, as she packed every pot, pan, plate, piece of cutlery and all the assorted odds and ends that Newton's Laws force into kitchen drawers and cabinets.

Roberta's books and computer were packed into boxes along with Ann Marie's clothing and tools. The modest belongings we had accumulated were systematically rearranged into various boxes. Our home was disassembled, leaving only a somewhat shabby house in its wake. While watching that process unfold, I was glad I chose to leave Kat's and my house unchanged when I left it.

Horace walked onto the front yard and picked up a stack of five crates of books to put in his truck.

"My God, Edna," I said, "that must weigh close to a thousand pounds!"

"I know. Poor Horace is weak as a kitten from being shot the other day, but I expect he'll recover shortly. He always does."

The years have been good to me. I have had the extraordinary pleasure of watching a gifted and talented child grow into a confident young woman. Billy allows me to teach a basic Business English class at the college, which is fairly well attended. Ann Marie has opened her own business making expensive wood furniture for wealthy clients with too much money and an appreciation of beauty. Roberta has become the center of my life. It makes me a bit sad to realize all that I forfeited with my first two children. Apparently, I have a knack for fatherhood.

Roberta is eighteen and going to Holy Cross of all places, next Fall, despite never attending public school a day in her life other than LWCC. All modesty aside, I did write her an extraordinary recommendation. Now in my twelfth year since Kat passed away, and I'm still patiently waiting to die. Ann Marie is fond of saying, "GW, you'll outlive us all!"

Of course I know she's mistaken.

EPILOGUE

*"H*ow was your first semester, Roberta?"

"All A's. After all those years with GW, most of the professors were easy."

"Well, I'm proud of you, honey. When are you coming home?"

"I'm flying in tomorrow. Will you be able to pick me up at the airport?"

"Of course."

"How's GW?"

"I don't know, baby. He's losing weight and seems awfully weak. He insists it's nothing and refuses to go to a doctor. I'm thinking about calling Horace and asking him to drag GW to a hospital."

"He'd never do it."

"I know, I know. 'Ever' man gots the right to live and die as he sees fit with no interference.'" She growled in her best Georgia drawl.

"Can I talk to him?"

"He's sleeping, say hi to him in person tomorrow."

Roberta rode the bus from Worcester to South Station in Boston, and took the subway to Logan Airport. The entire way she tried to come up with the perfect words for Hodge. The day dragged on and the air seemed to try to put her to sleep, as modern travelers can attest. Finally, she sat back in her seat with her head turned toward the window watching clouds and patches of land and water.

Roberta walked through the front door, dropped her duffel bag of laundry, and hugged George Hodge. She felt as if only bones and air occupied his clothes. His face was thin and sallow, but his eyes were bright.

"Tell me, Lady Crusader, what did you think of Professor Lite for Freshman English Seminar?"

"I don't want to hurt your feelings, GW, but at first he seemed witty and brilliant, but the more I listened to him, the less he had to say. I think he's an old windbag."

"Excellent! I'm glad you're able to see through that sort, it will be an invaluable skill if you are to obtain a worthwhile education."

After a light late dinner, George Hodge excused himself to go to bed. Ten minutes later Roberta knocked on his door and walked in. Hodge put down his worn copy of Dickens and said, "Sit down, Roberta."

She sat on the edge of his bed and looked at Hodge. "*A Tale of Two Cities*? Really?"

"I find comfort in books where I already know the ending."

"You're dying, aren't you?"

"Yes, I am. But I knew I would last long enough for this conversation, Roberta."

"I love you, GW."

"And I love you, Roberta. You have been a daughter, a granddaughter, a friend, a guide and a reason to live for me. You're perhaps the finest person I have ever known."

"You helped make me what I am, GW. You're the best

teacher and father I could ever have had."

"Thank you. And as a favor to me, Roberta, take it a little easier on your stepfather. Billy is a flawed man, as are we all, but he is kind, he is intelligent, and he is absolutely devoted to your mother."

"I know. He's okay; I just like to give him a hard time."

"You have to realize you won't meet many people as bright as you are, Roberta. Be patient."

"I'm going to miss you so much, GW."

"And I'm going to miss everything..."

CPSIA information can be obtained
at www.ICGtesting.com
Printed in the USA
LVOW12s0805130517
534405LV00001B/13/P